ABOVE A DISTANT
SKY SEEN

ANTHONY W. EICHENLAUB

ISBN: 978-1-950542-19-2

oakleafbooks.com

Cover Art by: Anthony W. Eichenlaub

❀ Created with Vellum

To all who have been invisible when they wanted to be seen or seen when they wanted to be invisible.

CHAPTER ONE

It started as a pinprick in the northern sky, broken from the billion stars by only the plodding movement of lumbering moons. The light shone like phosphorus fire as it arced across the upper atmosphere, streaking down, down, down toward the planet of Sky. Ash didn't breathe until it banked low across the glowing horizon and veered toward the colony of Edge.

Then, she knew it was the one.

"Just like you predicted," Hector said. She could sense his giant form next to her in the dark trench, smelling all handsome and perfect, but she couldn't see him. "This is going to work."

Ash Morgan wore slate-gray fatigues to better blend with the granite terrain. Her wild dark hair danced in the gentle wind, and she was glad for the darkness because it meant nobody could read the doubt on her face. She touched the button on the thin black trigger and mentally traced the long string of devices it would activate. This had to be perfect.

There hadn't been a shuttle in the six months since she'd faked her death, giving her plenty of time to over-think this very moment. Her plan was perfectly designed, assembled in exquisite detail, and soon to be perfectly executed. Best case, she'd end up with a functioning shuttle that would take her anywhere she wanted to go. Worst case, the AI Traverse would finally take that extra step to burn every single human off the face of the planet like lancing a boil.

"I don't think we're ready for this at all," she said.

Hector placed a big hand on her shoulder. "You'll do fine."

She looked down at the trigger. "I know *I* can do my part."

"Then what's the problem?"

"It's just that I think Simon's probably going to screw up," Ash whispered. "I'm not ready to see this kind of pressure break him."

Simon's voice came through the comm. "I can hear you, you know."

Ash shushed him. "Tobin said we should try to stay quiet."

Tobin said nothing, but a shadow not far away emitted a growl of frustration.

The shuttle from Traverse was a sleek thing, bright and shiny, with a wasp waist separating passenger compartments from cargo. It was invisible on the auto-mated detection system run by Traverse, ran almost completely silent through the night sky, and could self-destruct in under ten seconds. Ash and her team had never been able to build anything equivalent, even with their best materials printers. Even Seaside and Pyramid, the planet's longest-lived colonies, had never truly mastered flight, let alone space travel.

It was on Ash's to-do list, but she couldn't wait long enough to build her own. When it landed in a cloud of dust and ozone, Ash mashed the button.

Nothing.

Hector grumbled. Somewhere in the dark, Tobin swore. In seconds the new colonists would step out and the shuttle would fly away. Ash would have to wait for the next flight. If there ever was one. With luck, Traverse would simply abandon Edge. Their colonies had outgrown their purpose, after all. They were liabilities.

Tobin slid into the trench next to Ash. He wore the most stylish camouflage Ash had ever seen, but his sharp features were twisted into an expression near panic. "What are you waiting for?"

"It's not working."

The shuttle doors hissed, belching a cloud of steam.

"Give me that," Tobin said. He took the trigger, disengaged a clip on the side, and pressed the button.

The air buzzed with an electrostatic crackle that Ash felt on the back of her neck and the tops of her hands. Shuttle doors froze halfway up and the single foot that stepped on the ground stopped moving. The only motion was the slow drift of steam as the gentle wind tugged across the open landing pad.

"Go!" shouted Ash.

She leaped from the trench, Hector at her side. Across the pad, the Skyling Kett burst from another trench. Like all Skylings, he had the ridged nose and wicked claws. He also stood a head taller than even Hector and his mane of hair made him look like a wild animal. Beside him ran Palak, no less fierce with her corded muscle and short-cropped black hair.

Hector hit the shuttle first, found a good grip on the landing struts, and lifted. The giant Kett launched Palak atop the shuttle, where she attached a long cable to the hull. She gave the signal and Ash heard Del started the winch.

Hector heaved with all his might. Kett pulled. An inch. Two inches. Palak's winch went taut, and the whole shuttle tipped.

Ash scrambled underneath, followed closely by Simon. His lithe arms pulled his slender body forward. His brush with a Skyling mutation left him lean and strong. The barest nubs of ridges spotted his nose, but his perfect hair hadn't moved one inch.

"I can't read these labels!" Ash said.

"Fuel, tech port, data." Simon read the archaic symbols as if they were his native language. "Here, do this one, I'll work here."

Ash pulled her multitool from her belt and unscrewed a bolt holding the largest panel in place. Together, they loosened enough to peel away the black metal and reveal the dizzying array of ancient technology.

"Come on, Traverse," Ash said.

"One minute!" Tobin shouted, punching controls on his tablet.

"I thought we had five minutes," Ash shot back.

"Well, the field is unstable," Tobin said.

Palak, from inside the shuttle, said, "What did you do to these people?"

"Nothing!"

"They're all out cold." Palak motioned for Kett to help, so the big man abandoned the winch and lifted a passenger through the half-open shuttle door. "Get them out of here!"

Simon attached a data spike to a port under the shuttle. "This is different," he muttered. "It's all different."

"I knew it," Ash hissed under her breath.

He shot her the most scathing look he had ever managed to produce.

The shuttle shuddered.

"Mind the winch," she said, failing to keep the fear from her voice. The shuttle dropped an inch. If it fell, she and Simon would be grease stains and fantastic memories.

"Simon, which one do I pull?" Ash asked.

Simon read the labels, running down through each strange device and checking it against the feed on his datakey. "There," he said, not sounding anywhere near as sure as he ought to. "No, that one."

Ash clicked her multitool until it had the right attachment and worked furiously at the part. If he was right, this was the explosive device that would destroy the shuttle in the imminent self-destruct. She didn't have time to be properly careful with it, so she worked fast instead.

"Less time to screw things up," she muttered to herself.

"What?" asked Simon.

"If I rush, there's less time to make a mistake, so therefore less chance of a mistake."

"That's not how probability works!"

Kett growled as he hefted a passenger out of the shuttle. "The winch is failing."

Hector's face was a deep purple, his bulk struggling against the sheer mass of the shuttle. He had a bar propped under one rail, but it bent as his muscles failed and more pressure leaned on it.

"How are the cameras?" Ash shouted.

Palak said, "I'm busy." She dragged an unconscious passenger to the bunker. "I can't get them."

Tobin's fingers danced over the cracked screen of a tablet, the green light of its text dancing across his face.

"Del," shouted Ash.

"On it." Delilah Baxter jumped from the bunker by the winch with the pack of Ash's custom-designed lens caps. Del was an older woman with a dark jacket and heavy boots. The trifocal refraction in her glasses caught the light as she crossed the distance to the shuttle. She slapped a dome over each recording node. The inside of each dome depicted an image of the appropriate location in or around the shuttle. A cheap trick, but hopefully an effective one.

Palak dumped a passenger into a trench and ran back for another. Kett hefted two more on his shoulders and ran free.

Simon grabbed Ash's hand. "That's not the right

one."

Ash looked at the cylinder, now almost detached from the shuttle. "Then what is this?"

"I don't know."

"So, it *might* be the bomb?"

"No, it's definitely not."

"Can we call that fifty-fifty?"

"Ash!" Panic ran like a firestorm through Simon's voice. "It's that one!"

"Fine!" Ash switched tasks.

Hector made a sound like a wounded goose. The shuttle dropped another few inches.

"Ten seconds!" shouted Tobin.

"Buy us more time," yelled Simon. "Please."

Tobin didn't bother answering.

"Fine," said Ash. "Simon, get this thing out of here. Fast." She took a knife from her belt and tossed it to him.

"What?" Simon fumbled the tool, dropped his data spike, and generally made a mess of things. When he picked up the knife and pushed a button, blue flames wreathed the blade. "Oh." It was the knife that had belonged to Ash's mother. Dangerous to use on the shuttle's inner workings, but probably their best chance at removing the detonator.

Ash scrambled up through the partially open door just as the electric hum fell out of the air. Lights flickered in the shuttle's compartment, revealing Del as she attached the last of the video domes over a camera node. Ash ushered Del from the compartment and flopped down into one of the shuttle's empty pilot seats.

Kett dropped in beside Hector and helped lift, and together they kept the shuttle balanced. Palak dragged the last of the new colonists from the shuttle, a woman nearly twice Palak's size with intricate tattoos on her bare arms.

"Hey, Traverse," Ash said in her most charming voice. She removed a dome from a camera just above the pilot's seat.

The *T* logo on the screen spun silently for several seconds, then Traverse said, "Initiating self—"

"I'll stop you right there, big guy," Ash said. "I know standard procedure is to say, 'initiating self-destruct' whenever something goes wrong with the shuttle, but there's nothing wrong right now. Everything's in really good shape and nobody is even trying to steal any part of this technology."

The logo spun. "Sensors indicate—"

"Certainly not a theft in progress. There was a little bit of a bump when this shuttle landed, due to weather conditions, but automated systems are repairing things and we should lift off in just a few seconds."

"Diagnosis—"

"Indicates that everything's fine. There isn't even anybody inside the pilot compartment, which is great news. In fact, nobody's here at all, not even the corpse of someone who died six months ago. Can you believe that? Nobody died. You aren't talking to Ash Morgan, adventurer, microbiologist, and hero of the colony of Edge, and she is definitely not trying to stall you. You couldn't possibly be talking to her, because she died six months ago shortly after the Seasider attack. The colony is peaceful now, people are mostly all getting along again, and there's no reason to think that there shouldn't be piles of good experiments left for Edge to perform."

"Ash Morgan," said Traverse. "Registered as deceased."

"Yeah, you got me. We've been through a lot together, haven't we? You helped raise me, after all. Trained me in everything I know, from the biology that I'm so very good at to the loads of Earth lore I've picked up from your extensive media banks. In fact, it's totally cool that you're going to blow me up in a few seconds. That's basically everything I've come to expect from such a good friend, but can I ask you a question first?"

The logo spun three full rotations before Traverse responded. "Proceed."

"Thanks, buddy."

The shuttle lurched and Simon screamed high and loud. Hector and Kett strained under the effort to keep it from crushing him.

Ash swallowed back the panic rising in the back of her throat. It was all she could do to keep her fear from her voice, something she knew would trigger Traverse's warnings. One of the best ways to get a lie past Traverse was to not lie at all. "I'm scared, Traverse," she said, but she said it in a very calm voice, so that was probably okay. "I need to know something, and I want a real, honest answer."

Traverse said nothing.

"What is the purpose of all this?"

The logo spun for an eternity, during which Ash

9

dared not speak. There was only so much she could do to distract Traverse. She stared at the single, glass eye of its last remaining internal camera, keeping her face devoid of all expression.

"Got it!" shouted Simon.

In the corner of her eye, she saw her friend roll out from under the shuttle. She braced herself as Kett and Hector dropped it to the ground. The impact sent vibrations through her bones.

"What's the purpose, Traverse? How does it end?" Ash asked again. "This human experiment. The colonization of Sky, and the taming of a new world in the vast name of humankind. What does the end of the experiment look like?"

Outside, Simon and Del dropped the cylinder into a metal tube. The others ran back to the trenches, but Ash knew she didn't have time. The second she backed away, Traverse would trigger its self-destruct. She had to keep its attention, and she had to be there when it happened. If Simon had picked the wrong piece to detach, then she'd be dead. She wouldn't even be around long enough to regret her choices.

Not that she'd really regret this, anyway. She had to try, after all. This was their only chance to save the colony. Eventually, no matter what, Traverse would kill them all. Maybe they could limp along like the Pyramid or Seaside settlements, but the slow deaths those colonies faced weren't much better than the fast death Traverse had almost enacted before. No, they needed the shuttle. They needed a way to rescue the colonists still up on the ship, steal a datacore of

Traverse's research, and destroy the ship's dominance over Sky once and for all.

Ash asked once more, with resignation in her voice, "How does it end, Traverse?"

Simon pulled a trigger, and the cannon launched the cylinder high into the cool night air.

"Violently, Ash Morgan," said Traverse, its voice sounding surprisingly human. "It always ends violently."

The cylinder exploded, sending a crushing shock-wave downward. Ash's ears rang and her head went numb.

She scrambled from the shuttle and shouted, even though she couldn't hear her own voice. "Now, now! Pull it across!"

Kett and Hector ran, each pulling one corner of a massive tarp. Thousands of yards of synthetic cloth spread out over the landing pad. Ash grabbed an edge and scrambled with it over the shuttle. Above, smoke spread, carried east by the night's cool wind.

The tarp snagged on the shuttle, but she yanked it free, dropped down on the other side, and ran. They pinned the edges to the earth near the trenches.

On its top, they'd printed the image of a destroyed shuttle. From the sky, Traverse would see only ruins. Tobin scrambled the area's comm feed. The night went silent.

They had a shuttle.

"Well, team," Ash said, gathering them together, "now the real heist begins."

CHAPTER TWO

Ash raised her glass. "I propose a toast to celebrate a successful mission without any problems at all."

Simon raised his glass, hesitated, and said, "The shuttle almost crushed me, Ash."

"Almost."

Hector slapped Simon on the back. "Nice work back there."

Simon's brow furrowed. "What happened to the winch?"

Kett snorted. The glass of nectar he held looked tiny in his huge, clawed hand. The big man had changed over the past year, his body finally realizing its full potential, as one of the world's few healthy adult Skylings. The ridges of his nose helped him breathe in almost any atmosphere, his skin was hardened against the elements, and his teeth and claws made him impervious to all forms of social ridicule. "The gears stripped when the metal gave out." He tipped his glass toward Hector. "It's a good thing this guy was there."

They drank in Marta's cave, the same place Marta had long ago given birth to the strange child Skye, now transformed into Ash's underground hideout. It was filled with pilfered tech and was more than a little shady. A printer along one wall handled her material needs and she kept it attached to an isolated instance of Traverse.

"I can't believe you installed Traverse on your own hardware," said Simon.

Ash thumped the machine with her boot. "Traverse is a computer program. I can install an instance of it on a tiny system like this or on a giant system like the ship. It's all the same."

"I thought they were all different."

"And they're all different." She drank, as she often did when Simon got that bewildered look on his face. She looked around at her cave. Hector had excavated some new rooms, which had been her home ever since she'd faked her own death and set the gears rolling for her big mission: the downfall of Traverse. She raised her glass. "To the destruction of Traverse!"

Del sidled up next to Ash, "I helped you get the shuttle, kid, but that's as far as I go." Her eyes sagged with the kind of exhaustion that comes after a lifetime of bad news. "I'm out."

"I made you something," Ash said. She reached into her pack and withdrew a bulky pistol with a retro rocket-style barrel and battery pack.

Del pushed the barrel away. "Get your finger off the trigger, Ash."

"Don't worry, it's fake."

"I recognize an energy pistol when I see one. It's not going to change my decision."

Ash blinked at the woman. "But I need you."

"It is what it is," Del said, but she took the pistol. "I don't want you anywhere near this."

Ash felt as if sand were slipping between her fingers and reached for the one thing she could say that would convince everyone to help. When nothing came, she got up to go find another glass of nectar, but something must have been functionally wrong with the planet's gravity because she needed to sit immediately. Luckily, Hector returned with two drinks, so she snagged one.

Kett said, "The Seasiders demand that I step back as well. This isn't our fight. We have survived for generations at the base of the mountain, and we will continue our way of life."

Ash narrowed her eyes, trying to process the scary-looking man's growling accent. "Traverse ignores your people." Skylings would never be equal as long as Traverse ignored them. "You'll maintain your way of life, but you'll never conquer the world."

He leaned close and growled low, "This mission went terribly, Ash, and if you don't plan better for your trip to the station, then your team will die. We want no part in that. Think of Skye. He is nearly old enough to start a trade, but you'd risk his life for one shot at the AI?"

Sand. Fingers. Ash raised her glass in the air, "To quick thinking under pressure!" It earned a grumble from her remaining team.

She spun around slid along the bench to sit next to Tobin. Her momentum carried her a little too far, but she smoothly converted the extra movement into a conspiratorial lean. "Sorry about your tech, Tobin. I know it's hard being the smart one all the time when things fail." She leaned even closer.

Tobin leaned away. "You smell like a fermentation factory."

"What I'm saying is don't take it too hard."

He sighed. "This isn't the time or place to discuss this, Ash, and you aren't in any condition."

"I figure Traverse probably made some adjustments since the last shuttle. It knew we were coming."

"That's—actually probably correct." He eyed her suspiciously.

She winked at him. "And if it knew we were coming, then it probably has more plans than just that. I'm thinking horrible flesh-eating microbes or a new protein DNA trigger. It definitely caused the winch failure by messing with our engineering printers."

Tobin rubbed his chin. "The new colonists are in quarantine at the jailhouse. We'll run tests on them and see if they suffer any ill effects."

Ash waved it off. "Traverse isn't going to be so obvious."

"From what I hear, it once attempted to destroy Edge with a giant beam from the sky."

"A beam that nobody expected." Ash made a grand gesture that nearly knocked Tobin's drink off the table. "Like the disapproving gaze of God."

"That just accentuates the fact that we don't know

what we're getting into up there," Tobin said, "if we even go."

"Of course, we'll go. And we'll be fine. Today proved that we can handle last second changes to our plan."

"We don't *have* a plan."

"Sure, we do. We go up. We grab whatever we can. Smash everything else. Trigger the evacuation. Then, we come back down."

"Smash and grab?" Tobin took a big drink of his nectar. "We were promised a well-planned heist."

"It's grab *then* smash." When Tobin had no response to her excellent point, she asked, "What do you remember of the ship?"

"I was born on planet. Pyramid survived many generations before Traverse started starving us out."

"Well, *I* remember the ship." She peered at her drink, which had somehow become dangerously empty. "There are segments, each surrounded by void and spinning around the central sphere. They call those segments boroughs because that's what they called parts of a city back on Earth."

Hector sat at the table next to them and slid a new drink over to Ash. "Each borough is completely independent. People don't move between them unless it's to go into *retirement*."

"Which is another word for when Traverse murders people and renders them into constituent elements."

"I've read about this," Tobin said. "Connecting

conduits between boroughs are heavily guarded, and every borough is slightly different."

Hector said, "When I was young, everyone was very nice. They taught us that there was always a reason to help other people, even when we didn't want to."

"In your borough, they fed you a constant flow of sunshine and rainbows," Ash said. "My borough was all about invention, innovation, and competition. If we can figure out how many human virtues there are, maybe we can figure out how many boroughs we'll need to free."

Tobin rubbed his eyes. "You don't know how many boroughs there are?"

"I mean, a lot, probably," Ash said.

"But you don't know."

"Five at least."

Tobin looked to Hector. He shook his head.

"Maybe seven?" Ash took a long pull of her nectar. The orange stuff had a sour aftertaste, but she loved the way it warmed her fingers and made her toes tingle. "It's an odd number for sure. But it won't matter once we've taken the core instance. That's the only place that can communicate with all of the boroughs at once. Nodes only talk to five adjacent boroughs."

"It isn't the core I'm worried about," Tobin said. "It's everything leading up to that point."

"You're probably going to tell me we need a really detailed plan."

"First of all," Tobin said, "it's in space. You need to *go* there. Yes, yes, I know that's why you got the shuttle, but we don't know anything about flying a shuttle. Do you know what that means?"

"Things get really detailed? And planned?"

"It means you need to fool Traverse into taking us. Traverse thinks the shuttle is destroyed, so when it comes online, it'll know something's wrong."

Ash nodded, wide-eyed.

"Then, you can't just hit an evacuation order and expect all the colonists to survive. You're going to need to warn them and execute an orderly evacuation. Work through channels to notify all of the colonists that they'll be moving planetside."

"I was just going to mash the button," Ash mumbled.

"People will die either way. You have to accept that when you make this decision." Tobin drummed the table with his immaculate fingernails. "You'll need to be able to move around the ship, which is not something just anyone can do."

"How do you know this again?"

"He read a book," said Hector.

"I read the design documents Simon found in the Archives," agreed Tobin. He got along entirely too well with Hector, and it was starting to get annoying. "There are details you wouldn't guess just by your experience aboard the ship. Things that were hidden from you, but not hidden from the archivists."

"I read all that." Skimmed, really. "None of this will work without Simon's help." Ash raised her glass in the air. "To Simon!" But Simon wasn't there anymore. In fact, everyone but Hector and Tobin had left. "To

Simon," she muttered again, and she polished off the last of her nectar.

"That was my drink," Tobin said.

"Oh, sorry." Ash slid his glass back to him and picked up her own.

"Assuming you can even get to the core, there will be security in place. The greatest AI ever designed by mankind protects its core jealously. Only the original architects were granted access to the central core."

"Well, we'll just ask them to do it, then."

Tobin stared at her. "They were alive thousands of years ago."

"So were you."

He opened his mouth to protest, then shut it again. He wasn't thousands of years old, but he had been in stasis for a millennium. She really needed to study how stasis worked.

She said, "They would have passed on the permissions to their children. No architect would want their creation to fall to ruin just because they died. It's a legacy thing."

Tobin continued, "Regardless, we need to execute a detailed plan as quickly as possible. The more complicated we get, the more likely Traverse will get upset and shut us down completely."

"You keep talking about Traverse like it's a person."

"If it's a person then it's a murderer."

Ash's head was spinning, so she took a sip of her nectar, which had never worked before and certainly did not work this time. "We'll have help from residents on the ship. Hector is pretty good at convincing people to do stuff."

"I listen to them," Hector said.

"It's magic," said Ash. "But he does it, and that's why I need him along. You're our tech guy, and Simon is our interpreter. He knows all the written languages Traverse has used here in the archives. Del used to do work maintenance on the ship when she was young, so she knows how to move through the ship if we can disable security. Kett will be around for two reasons. Grunt work that Hector can't do alone and for when we need a presence that Traverse doesn't believe is human. He's practically invisible because Traverse is a *huge* racist."

"Now you're the one talking about Traverse like it's a person."

"Computers can have bias."

"I might be able to exploit that," said Tobin, scratching his chin.

"Didn't Kett say he wasn't coming?" asked Hector.

"He was just kidding," Ash whispered. "Traverse can't see Seasiders, so he'll be like a giant, stealthy kitten. Who could resist that?"

"Why are you bringing Palak?" Tobin asked.

"That spear she always carries is critical to the mission, Tobin."

"That doesn't seem likely if things go according to plan," said Tobin.

"Every good heist has contingency plans." She drank the last of her nectar and pushed the glass away. "Sometimes things don't go according to plan."

"Like today," Tobin said.

"We had it under control." She absolutely had not. "All I had to do was have a little chat with Traverse, and things worked out fine."

"A little chat that revealed to Traverse that you're still alive. Part of the plan had you faking your death. I remember it. You didn't need to be so theatrical, did you?"

"My reveal had to be convincing and confusing," Ash explained. "That's Traverse's biggest weakness. If you're confusing enough, it just locks up trying to figure you out."

"And now you've played that card. We aren't even off planet."

"Yeah." It was a problem. She had always had a special relationship with Traverse, so faking her own death was supposed to give her an edge when she finally revealed herself.

It had worked. She credited their survival with the machine's delayed response in handling the recalculations necessary when it realized she was still alive. That, and her clever wit and quick thinking. Now, though, she wouldn't be able to count on the surprise. She stared at her empty glass.

Ash swiped through the documents on her tablet. Ship data architecture designs appeared on the screen, partially obscured by the spiderweb of cracks. It showed the hierarchy of authority amongst the different instances, from the lowest versions planetside to the most powerful core instance. "We can do this," she said with no conviction in her voice.

He stood and walked to the door. "Your team has left you. We need to think of other options."

Ash raised her glass high. "To the greatest heist this planet has ever known."

But there was nobody to hear but Hector, and he hardly counted since he would support her no matter what.

CHAPTER THREE

"THAT'S EASY," Ash said to Hector as they toiled on the shuttle under the massive tent for the fifth day in a row. "All they want is to destroy Traverse, plunder the databanks for the genetic data of a million Earth creatures, and return to Sky in a fiery blaze of glory."

"That's what *you* want, hon," Hector said.

"The blaze of glory is optional."

"Ash."

"How am I supposed to know what the members of the council want? They're entirely different people, and I haven't figured out how to read minds yet."

"Yet?"

"It's seriously a long ways off. Five years."

Hector's wrench slipped and he slammed his knuckles into the metal shielding. "You're not really trying to read people's minds are you?"

"It's probably a destructive process. I could maybe mind-control them. Like puppets."

"Ash."

"It helps that you have all that neurotech in you from Pyramid, but it depends on how it's connected to your nervous system." She tapped one of the golden nodes nestled in his matted brown hair. "Just plug in here..."

Hector sucked on his injured knuckles. "I think you're trying to do too much."

Ash punched through the controls on her tablet. It was the only tablet to ever give her a partial override of Traverse's inner workings, but half the screen was lost in a web of cracks and the power source failed randomly. "I'll just ask you next time I want to know what you're thinking."

"Did you come up with that solution yourself?"

"Simon helped."

This drew a soft chuckle from the big guy.

"I'm not doing too much. I'm doing too little." Ash chewed her lip. "I figured it out, you know. The planetary-scale balance equation. DNA mathematics. Everything." She watched yellow alert messages scroll past on the tablet.

"You've told me this before."

"I know, but it's really true. The solution to everything." Orange warnings flashed on the screen, and Ash paused the feed to read them. The tablet didn't have direct connection to Traverse, but it had enough logic to parse her words for certain keywords. "Homeostasis," she said, and the messages turned purple.

Hector set his wrench down and looked at Ash.

"Did you use those words in town like I asked?" she asked.

"Every day last month."

"Homeostasis is the big one." The messages flashed purple again when she said it. "Traverse seems to get excited whenever we talk about finding a way to balance Sky's ecosystem. It's like Traverse's holy grail. The end mission."

"I'm aware. Balance the planet and life will sustain itself."

Ash ran a hand along the sleek lines of the shuttle. Its cold fiber surface felt like glass under her rough fingertips. She hefted the multitool in her hands. The solid heft of it always brought her comfort, like having every solution to every problem right at her fingertips. Her multitool could be anything from a hammer to a data spike to a fingernail clipper. "There's so much to do, Hector," she finally said. "So much to test."

They worked for a while in silence. Ash configured the modified printer. Hector tinkered with the crystalline fuel cells that would power the shuttle on its voyage back up into space. They both wore green canvas overalls with a planet surrounded by seven moons sewn onto the shoulder.

Ash said, "I think a full brain scan might work."

Hector said nothing.

"I mean, it would still be a destructive scan, but there's a lot you can learn if you're willing to destroy something completely."

"We should go."

They packed up their tools and bundled them out of the shuttle to the small bunker at the edge of the tent. Late afternoon sunlight still filtered through the false image of the destroyed shuttle. The trench bunkers, which they had originally built to hide in while the shuttle landed, now served as a way station between the actual shuttle proper and the rest of the world. They could only come and go during the hours of the day when the ship fell below the horizon. Moving anywhere near the site during the times when Traverse could watch them from above was far too risky.

They circled around the colony to Little Seaside, where Ash's old tiny house stood in the middle of a vast network of heavily fortified cubes. The squarish architecture was a throwback to the red clay structures which made up most of the Seaside ruins—the ancient colony down at the base of the mountain that had been long since abandoned by the Seasiders themselves. Little Seaside, here in the last waning hours of the day, bustled with activity. Food stalls sold fresh cooked meat and vegetables served over aromatic noodles or rice.

"You want some?" she asked Hector with noodles dangling from her mouth. "It's really spicy."

"I don't like spicy food."

"Of course, you do. You just don't know it yet." She scooped up some noodles with her chopsticks and stabbed them at his face.

He laughed and dodged away. "Nope!"

She pursued. Ate noodles. Scooped up more, then chased after him. "Spicy noodles!"

Hector pulled up short and Ash slammed into his back. Noodles flew everywhere.

They wove through the tangled network of streets, past the stubby trees of the garden district and the flowing grasses that swarmed with guinea pigs, moles, and a tiny breed of ocelot that somehow managed to only rarely take down a guinea pig.

They met Simon on his way into the Archives, and Ash marveled at how dapper the man looked with his glossy hair and sharp suit. As they all stepped into the round building, the tap of his wildly impractical shoes echoed in the resounding emptiness.

On the way down, Hector whispered, "Just try to remember what *they* want, okay?"

"Blaze of glory?" Ash whispered back.

Hector took both her hands in his and looked her straight in the eyes. "You're nervous," he said.

Ash closed her eyes and drew a long deep breath.

The doors opened deep underground to a room buzzing with energy. Papers and plans and people choked the huge conference room: the results of all the machinations Ash led in her quest to finally take down Traverse. On the far side of the giant stone table, Olympia argued with Kett and Tobin while Palak, her brother Harish, and Del watched on. There were a dozen other people that Ash didn't recognize.

Olympia said, "The new colonists haven't finished their quarantine."

Tobin said, "We have dormant DNA that is activated by rogue proteins. It could be triggered at any point by anything Traverse sent down."

"That's not what quarantine protects us from," said Olympia. "You're being disingenuous, Tobin."

"He's not," growled Kett. "We need to scrap this whole thing and find other ways to move forward."

A murmur went through the crowd.

Olympia turned to Ash, "I'm glad you could make it." The tension in her thin smile almost didn't find its way into her words. "There are some decisions to be made and we'd like the status of the shuttle."

Ash stepped up to the table and scanned the people there. Far more attended the meeting than she'd expected, but she could adapt. She spotted the plump food scientist Juliette leaning back in her chair, arms folded across her lap. Tall thin Jasper and wild-haired Leonard also provided friendly faces. If she spoke just to them—just to the people she knew—maybe she could manage to convince them of what needed to be done.

"The shuttle can launch any time," she said. She shot a glance at Hector, who nodded his affirmation. "We're behind schedule because there was damage to the shuttle when we removed the self-destruct detonator, but the main printer is installed, and the info-jacks are configured to fool Traverse's basic systems to force docking. Other modifications aren't complete but should be ready in another week."

The statement triggered another murmur in the crowd and a disappointed look from Olympia.

Olympia tapped on the table with one long, polished fingernail. "We pulled seven colonists out of the shuttle, Ash. They've been in quarantine for days."

Ash said, "Let me question them."

Olympia snapped, "No."

"Cursory questioning shows that they have a better understanding of the ship than anyone who has come down previously," said Tobin.

"That sounds"—Ash searched for the right word —"perfect."

"I'm not letting you near them," said Olympia. "It's too risky."

Hector took Ash's hand in his. His comforting warmth triggered something in her, and she knew that what they said next would be bad.

Tobin touched a folder lying on the table next to a couple of Seasiders. "We've assembled an alternative plan and shared it with the group. It's far simpler, with an almost guaranteed chance of success. It saves all of our colonies, destroys the threat of Traverse forever, and frees our people."

A tingle of irritation prickled the back of Ash's neck. They'd gone behind her back to make a plan that wouldn't get them what they needed. Worse, Hector knew this was coming. She pulled her hand away from his.

"Ash," Hector whispered.

"We thought we'd have you in to speak before the council puts this to a vote," Olympia said. "There are benefits to both plans, but we'd like to hear them articulated, and you know there are details that we haven't figured out in your plan."

"You're going to skip the evacuation," Ash said, peering now at the plans on the board.

"It's less risk," said Tobin.

Ash closed her eyes and took a deep breath. The room smelled of stale sweat and flowery perfume, but more than anything it smelled of the cold burnt scent of deceit. She thought of destroying Traverse, of plundering the databanks for new organisms with which to populate the world, of returning in a blaze of glory. Those were things *she* wanted. Tobin's plan lacked the blazes of glory. It lacked any plundering of databanks. It lacked any rescuing of thousands of living human beings existing in ignorance aboard the ship.

"You'll all be murderers," she said without opening her eyes. "Untold thousands, maybe millions, live aboard that ship, and you'll be plunging it into the atmosphere to burn in a horrible, fiery death. Vote for Tobin's plan of simple destruction and you'll be murdering everyone up there."

"Many would escape," said Tobin. "Automated evacuations would happen."

"Many wouldn't. They would have no warning."

"We have no way to absorb millions," Tobin said quietly. "It would be a slow death for us all."

Ash locked eyes with Olympia. "When we met our friends from Anvil, we could have easily killed them. We didn't. Because of that, we gained a hundred new flavors of nectar, food we'd never dreamed of, and advancements in mechanical engineering that would have taken us decades." She turned to Tobin. "You, Tobin, wouldn't even be here if Hector hadn't taken the time to wake all of your people safely from Pyramid. You'd have all died at the end of time, frozen in your stasis pods. From you, we gained materials science that would have taken generations to discover. The Seasiders gave us farming techniques that will allow us grow our colony."

"But not quickly enough," said Tobin.

"We don't know that. You're speculating on our ability to handle something we don't even know is a problem. There may be dozens of boroughs up there, but how many are populated? Maybe not even half. Maybe not even a third. You can't murder them all just because you think there *might* be too many of them."

The room's silence rang in her ears, and only then did she realize that she had been yelling. Her vocal cords ached with the remnants of raw emotion. She forced her next words out calm and smooth. "This will be our greatest moment. Our legends will live on long after we're gone, and the planet will be saved. Don't you understand? My plan saves everything."

When nobody else spoke up, Olympia said, "Let's put this to a vote." When nobody protested, she said, "All in favor of Ash's plan."

A smattering of scientists raised their hands. Hector, Kett, and Simon sided with her, but too few of the others did the same.

"And Tobin's plan."

Significantly more scientists voted for Tobin. Ash seethed. She sat at the table and placed her hands palm down on its cold surface. "Let's see this plan."

Many of the scientists filtered out of the room, leaving a smaller group to finalize the details. In one week, they would send the shuttle up with a small crew. They would deliver a dataspike to one of the boroughs, and from there the corruption would spread. The central system would be overridden, and a cataclysmic shutdown of Traverse's central core would destroy everything.

"You discovered a flaw in the design," Ash said.

Tobin leaned forward and pointed to the diagram of Traverse's interconnected instances. "If we can take one, it'll cascade to the rest."

"What if the others around it detect the anomaly and override it?"

"It'll work."

"Unless Traverse locks down into protected mode," Ash said, now understanding why their two plans were probably incompatible. "This still works if we're careful in how we execute my plan."

"Ash, you've never been careful."

"It might happen."

"Some of the people aboard the ship will have time to evacuate," said Tobin grimly.

"But most won't know where to go," said Ash. "They'll seed the planet with their corpses."

"Then we have one week to solve that problem. The AI can always tell when people are stressed or lying. How would you get them that information without alerting Traverse?" Tobin looked meaningfully to her, as if expecting a response.

"I'll figure it out," she said. "Someone will need to deliver that message."

When they had finished, Olympia touched Ash's shoulder and said, "Thank you."

"For what?"

"You could have made that a lot uglier for us."

"Yeah." She could have. She should have.

Olympia left with Tobin in the next elevator.

Kett, Hector, and Simon were the only ones left waiting for the elevator. When it arrived, they shuffled in, and Ash pushed the button.

Halfway up, she said, "There's a launch window tomorrow morning just as Traverse dips below the horizon."

They stood in silence for several excruciatingly long seconds.

Ash glanced at Hector. He sighed and said to Kett, "I know you don't care that Traverse won't activate lights or doors for you. You consider those things useless. Same with screens since your people transfer knowledge via stories. Access to Traverse's media would endanger your way of life. Your culture." Hector placed a hand on Kett's shoulder. "But I've heard you complain about how Traverse won't print nutritional supplements for your children. I've heard you talk about how dangerous it is near automated worksites when the robots won't even slow for you. Your people— those who have started the transformation—find themselves cut off from the jobs they should be best at because they can't work alongside Traverse's machines." Hector looked the man right in the eyes. "Do this for them. For *their* future."

As the elevator door opened, Kett said, "I'm in."

"Magic," Ash whispered.

CHAPTER FOUR

A YOUNG MAN with brown hair and a square jaw stepped forward to the transparent barrier at the center of the crowded jailhouse. "Let me get this straight. You're not here to let us out of this quarantine zone, but if one of us volunteers for an extremely dangerous mission you'll let that person out, but only long enough for that person to risk their lives doing something, somewhere, using some skills that you think we all have."

Ash peered at the man. "That's about right."

"Doesn't that undermine this whole quarantine excuse?"

"Not at all."

"But you won't tell us what the skill is that you need, and you won't tell us why it's so dangerous."

He was getting it. "So, you're in?"

The man blinked at her slowly. Ash got an uncanny vibe off of the guy, and she started to think that maybe these new colonists weren't a perfect fit for her team after all.

"I'll do it," said a woman in the far corner. The other new colonists stepped aside to reveal the speaker. Tight, corded muscles flexed as the big woman pushed herself up from the flimsy chair. The sleeves of her powder-blue coveralls were rolled up to reveal a thick network of gray tattoos on olive skin. The big woman fixed Ash with eyes so bright they appeared golden in the harsh lights of the interview room. In three long strides, she stepped up to the barrier. "Just tell me where to sign."

"We don't really sign things in Edge. There's a tradition of honesty, and—"

The woman slammed her open palm on the glass. "I'm ready to get out of here."

"But Lace," said the man. "You know we were warned—"

Lace's upper lip twitched. "I don't care. I'll do what she wants if it'll get me out of this box."

"It's a pleasure to meet you, Lace." Ash's voice sounded tiny against the hard barrier, and she couldn't tell if the woman had even heard her. "I'm Ash Morgan."

After a pause, Lace said to the man, "I told you, Paul, I can't stand this place."

"You don't even know what she wants."

Lace turned to Ash. "Are you going to tell me what this is for?"

Ash folded her arms. "Just assume it's the worst thing you can imagine."

The big woman placed a hand on the man's

shoulder and looked him straight in the eyes. After a pause, she nodded.

Once they were on the wide, rugged path that circled Edge, Lace said, "Paul wasn't wrong, you know. Everything you people have done since we arrived on planet has been dodgy."

Ash said, "We're going to use your shuttle to go back up to the ship."

Lace stopped. "Is that so?"

"We'll come back down when we're done. It shouldn't even take all that long."

The big woman followed with a sour expression on her face. "I thought it was supposed to be some kind of paradise down here."

"Oh, it is. There are guinea pigs everywhere."

"What exactly do you mean by guinea pigs?"

"The food is great. We're basically free to pursue whatever research we want, even though certain paths are definitely encouraged."

"Are you talking about experimenting on humans?"

"Well, there's human neural modification. It's not really encouraged, but some of the scientists from Pyramid have done some incredible research." Ash scrambled up a sloped slab of granite and watched as Lace mounted the whole thing in two steps. "Astrophysics, on the other hand, is definitely discouraged by Traverse, and nobody I know is particularly good at it."

"What exactly are you expecting of me?"

"Food science is really a thing now. Plenty of human experimentation there. Don't tell Juliette that I said so, but I'm pretty sure it's the best science. I wish I had studied it when I was younger. I'm a microbiologist, by the way, but I dabble in other fields."

"Great."

Ash stopped when she saw a familiar figure sitting on a granite outcrop. "Hold up. We have to wait here for a few minutes."

Lace opened her mouth as if she were going to say something, but then closed it again.

Ash gestured for Lace to stay and approached the boy. "You got the message."

Skye, the first Skyling Ash had ever known, watched her with his golden yellow eyes. "Can I come with?" he asked with his growling accent. He had grown so much during the last year that Ash had to remind herself that he was younger than he looked.

"I'm sorry, Skye," she said. "It's too dangerous."

He jumped from the ledge and landed hard enough that his boots send rocks flying. "I'm bored."

Ash bit back words that she knew would make everything bad. Instead, she said, "You're not old enough," which made everything worse.

Rage flushed his cheeks. "Why don't you think I can do anything?"

"You're just a kid."

"I'll *always* be just a kid to you," he snarled.

"Yes!" Ash stepped forward and pulled him into a hug. "Yes, you will."

After a brief show of resistance, he melted and hugged her back. "Be safe."

"I will." She absolutely would not be. "I promise."

They talked for several minutes, and Skye gave her

updates on everything in town. When he finished, they hugged again, and he ran back toward the town.

Ash said to Lace, "You can ask as many questions as you want. We're outside Traverse's hearing here, so I can tell you whatever you need."

A muscle in Lace's square jaw tensed.

"How well do you know your way around the ship?" Ash asked.

Lace sat on the granite slab. "Some of us got access to move around the whole ship in the past few years. That gave me a pretty good idea of the layout, but if you're looking to break into something, I don't know that I can help."

The whole ship. This was better than Ash had hoped. "That's exactly the skill we need," Ash said. "What a perfect coincidence." She wondered why the new colonists had that access. "Do you know how to get to the core?"

Lace hesitated. The knuckles of her folded hands turned white. "We helped maintain the core recycler. Morgan, what are you up to?"

Ash squared up against the woman. With Lace seated, their heads were on the same level. "I'll let you out of this if you want, Lace. I wasn't lying about this being dangerous. We have a plan. A good one."

The big woman didn't speak for a very long time. Finally, she said, "And now you have a shuttle."

"How many people still live on the ship?"

"Hard to say," Lace said.

"Do you think it's more than a million?"

Lace didn't grace that with an answer.

"Probably not, huh? What do you think it would take to evacuate?"

"What?"

A chime sounded from Ash's multitool. "It's time." She turned on her heel and walked briskly along the path. Along the way, they met Hector and Simon.

Simon blinked up at Lace. "You the new recruit?"

"I suppose so."

Palak and Del arrived as the team sank into the trench closest to the edge of the tent. Del motioned Ash close. "Palak explained to me what you need. I don't know if I can do this, Ash."

Ash took the older woman's hands in her own. "You're already here, so I think you know that you can."

"What Ash means to say," said Hector, "is that we forgive you. For everything you did and for almost destroying the Anvil colony. You don't have to do this for us to get forgiveness."

A pained expression pinched Del's face. Then she said, "All right. I'll do my best."

"You won't regret this," Ash told Del.

"I already do."

"Where is Kett?" Palak asked.

"Picking up something from Tobin's lab," Ash said.

"Olympia's not going to be happy about you leaving early," said Simon.

Ash gave him a hard look. "She's not happy about anything, Simon. I thought you'd figured that out by now."

He said, "Well, she's going to be extra upset about this."

Ash led the team through a narrow trench, pausing to make sure Lace followed. The woman squeezed through the narrowest part and made it to the tented space where the shuttle still lay open among the scattered debris of their equipment.

"Six hours," said Ash in her best impersonation of an authority. "Launch window's narrow this time around, so we're going to need to be ready."

Lace stood awkwardly, slightly hunched so that she could stay under the tent.

Ash flipped a switch on a panel near the aft end of the shuttle. She disabled her own comm. "Run dark, everyone." She watched as the others all switched off their units until the device showed only one transmission. "All right," she said, "who's holding out?"

The others patted themselves down, looking for a stray bit of technology that might still be transmitting. Ash didn't want anyone tracking their location, especially if Traverse started to realize that something was going on.

"Come on, people."

Simon climbed into the shuttle. "Automated systems in the shuttle might be running a boot sequence."

Del clapped Lace on the back and said, "You looking for some work?"

Lace glanced at the pistol on Del's hip. "I still don't know what the plan is."

"Good. Help me load this feedstock. We don't know what we'll need up there, so a variety of molecular feed for the printer is critical to the mission."

The two women worked on organizing the boxes and biopacks, rearranging pieces until they fit snugly in the cargo bay. Ash helped Hector reattach deflection plating on the underside of the shuttle. If they planned on returning to Sky, they were going to need the craft in as solid a shape as possible. Simon deciphered a series of messages on the shuttle's console, trying to disable to final comm signal while Palak packed and repacked a variety of weapons.

A few hours later, nearly half of the scattered innards of the shuttle were packed away. Kett arrived with a bundle under his arm. "Tobin's suits," he said. "Ready a week early."

Ash stuffed one of the suits into her pack. "That is just so exactly like Tobin, isn't it?"

"What is?" said Tobin, pushing his way under the flap of the tent.

Ash shot Kett a scowl. "You let him follow you here?"

Kett gave an apologetic shrug and wandered off to store the suits.

Tobin pushed past Ash. "What is the meaning of all this? What are you doing here?"

"We're definitely *not* getting ready to launch in a few hours," Ash said.

Tobin stared at her, his jaw working soundlessly. Without another word, he turned on his heel and stalked away. "I'm reporting this to the council."

Ash caught Lace peering at her through narrowed eyes and flashed an innocent smile.

The next hours passed in a rush. Palak argued with

Del about storage solutions. Hector grunted assent every time Ash gave him a new task, but his grunts became less amiable as the night went on.

"We want to launch while Traverse is below the horizon," Ash explained to Lace. "That way we're on the drift for most of the trip while we're visible. Once we're close, we trigger the docking sequence. We're pretty sure once that happens Traverse won't shoot us out of the sky."

"Pretty sure?" Lace asked.

"Like, really almost positive."

"Great."

Hector took Lace around to introduce the team. "Ash here is the brains of the operation. We're almost certain she has plans and backup plans for everything."

"I'm mostly just lucky," Ash tossed her multitool in the air and failed to catch it. She winced and left it on the crate where it landed next to her mother's blue knife, as if she had meant to put it there.

Hector pointed across the clearing where Del organized the last remaining molecular feedstock. "Del over there is..."

"She's a murderer," Ash whispered.

"Former murderer," Del shouted from across the way.

"She also has exceptionally good hearing," said Ash. "Like, *really* good hearing."

"Maybe you're just too loud," said Palak.

"Palak is another murderer," said Ash. "But I don't think she's sworn off the prospect of more murder."

Lace frowned. "This mission involves a lot of killers."

"I like to leave my options open," said Ash.

Hector pointed to the Seasider in the group. "Kett and I are muscle. We lift stuff. Sometimes we put it back down."

Kett bared his sharp teeth. Lace didn't seem at all surprised by the fact that they had a monster on their team.

Lace nodded to Simon. "What about you?"

"Translation," he said. "I'm here to interpret the written languages used by Traverse."

She grunted. "Some of them are pretty strange. Have you run into the pseudo-Aztec?"

Simon blinked slowly.

Lace said, "It's the one with the pictograms, but not the Egyptian one."

"Vertical or horizontal?"

Lace narrowed her eyes. "It's really more of a whole picture kind of thing."

"Are you a linguist, then?" Simon suddenly seemed fascinated by the big woman.

"Well, it was either study that or get good at murder. I didn't know what would be hiring."

Unsure if that was supposed to be a joke from the otherwise serious woman, Ash chuckled quietly and backed away.

Thunder rolled across the sky, followed by a heavy silence. Orange light played across the outside of the tent.

Before Ash could ask what was happening, Tobin

burst in under the tent flap flanked by Olympia and Jasper. Tobin clutched a stunner in his hand. The end of the two-foot rod crackled with electricity and menace.

"I came here to stop you, Ash," said Tobin taking a step forward, "but plans have changed. We need to leave now."

"What?" Ash's brain reeled. "Why?"

"Edge is under attack," said Olympia.

CHAPTER FIVE

"WHAT WAS THAT?" Palak asked when another boom
shook the tent.

"You have to go," said Olympia through gritted
teeth. She led Simon by the elbow toward the shuttle.
"Now."

"But—"

"Of course, I knew you were doing this," Olympia
said. "Now move."

Simon stood beside the shuttle. "I love you," he
said.

"I love you too, Simon," Olympia said for a second,
her steely exterior melted, and she held him close.

"Load the rest of this," Ash shouted to Palak. "I
don't care where it goes but get it inside. Now!" She
pointed to Tobin. "Help her."

To her absolute surprise, he obeyed. He powered
off the stunner and clipped it to his belt.

"Del!" Ash shouted. "Palak, bring the spear I gave
you."

Palak shot Ash an annoyed look. Her spear was already strapped to her back.

A nearby explosion rattled Ash's bones and lit up the tent. Closer this time. The tarp above them flapped furiously as the sky went dark once again.

Palak and Tobin crammed crates into the cargo section, lashing them down with free cord. Kett climbed into the cockpit and started the power-up sequence. Simon scrambled to gather more equipment to shove into cargo.

Ash ran through the trenches as the sky thundered above. She burst into the staging bunker and ran into Hector as a popcorn of smaller explosions crackled above.

"Go!" she shouted. "Get to the shuttle."

He ran. Ash scrambled to the bin and grabbed for her multitool, but it wasn't where she left it. A spike of panic stuttered her heart. She needed that tool. Another low thump sounded somewhere far away, and orange light washed over the canvas above.

There! She grabbed the tool, stuffing it in a pocket. She didn't have time for anything else, so she ran.

A crack-boom shredded the tarp, sending flaps of burning cloth into the wind. The sky flared with a thousand streaks of light. Olympia passed her in the trench, and the two women made eye contact.

"I'm trusting you," said Olympia.

"I know." Ash pushed past and came up under the tent. "Where is it coming from?"

"The sky," said Hector. "Everywhere. It's a meteor shower."

They both looked up as the wind shredded the last remnants of tarp. Smoke clouded the black sky. Meteors flashed in the east, with larger flares followed by booming explosions.

"Traverse did this," Ash said. It had to be the AI.

Hector didn't answer. Ash waved him toward the shuttle. Tobin loaded the last of the supplies. Lace crawled through the narrow passage between cargo and passenger areas. Kett sat in the pilot seat with a bewildered look on his face.

"The launch window is opening," Ash shouted. "Get this thing in the air! Everyone, buckle down."

Shuttle engines hummed in response.

A meteor struck one of their bunkers, and rocks pelted the side of the shuttle. A flash that ate the whole sky shook the whole mountain.

Rocks flew past Ash like a thousand bullets. Simon leaped from the shuttle and tackled Hector to the ground. The shuttle lifted from the earth and hovered. Ash jumped in.

"Get in!" She shouted, waving them both back toward the shuttle.

But Hector stumbled. Something was wrong. He looked at her with dazed, unfocused eyes. Blood covered his hand and soaked his shirt. Her heart stuttered to a stop at the sight of him injured.

The shuttle lifted higher, lurched to one side, then righted itself. Kett swore and wrestled the controls. Del jumped into the open passenger door. Her energy pistol hung at her hip and her glasses shone in the fiery light.

"I'm fine," Hector said, dabbing at a wound in his chest. Something had slashed across the top of his left pectoral muscle, deep enough that blood flowed from it. "I'll be fine."

Every plan had backups, Ash knew. And all the good backup plans had backups. It wasn't like she didn't plan on changing course halfway through. She knew that things would change, requirements would need to be reworked and reconfigured for the best opportunity at success. The most successful organisms in wild Earth were the ones that could adapt to any amount of environmental change, and she'd always designed her plans to do the same.

"I can't," she choked through the tightness in her chest. "I can't do this without you."

Tobin shouted from the back of the shuttle, but his words were lost in the roar of another meteor. She had no backup for this. Hector and Simon were both wounded. Attacks rained down from the sky. They needed to leave immediately, but...

Hector. Ash looked him in the eyes. He focused and met her right back. She knew that he wanted nothing more than to accompany her up to Traverse so that he could protect her from whatever she found there.

But she couldn't drag him to his death.

The sky flashed orange fire, and without another word, Ash reached for the shuttle door.

"Get Simon to safety!" Ash shouted at Hector. "I love you!"

She couldn't hear what he said in reply, but it was probably very romantic.

Simon and Hector collapsed backward, down into the protection of the trench.

"Go," Ash choked back a sob. "Go."

Ash closed the shuttle door and collapsed into a seat.

The shuttle launched upward into the sky. Ringing in Ash's ears faded enough that she started to better hear the voices around her.

Palak shouted, "What's happening out there?"

Kett, from the cockpit, said, "Hold on!" The shuttle lurched left and dropped a hundred feet.

Ash felt a strange vibration through the soles of her feet. "Is it supposed to sound like this?"

"Buckle it, Ash," said Del from directly behind her.

"I'll buckle it when I get some answers." Ash twisted around to face Del. "And what are they saying back there? I still can't hear very well."

Del gripped Ash's harness and said, "Buckle this. You can talk all you want, but please consider shutting up and thinking for once."

Ash locked the five-point harness around herself. It fit uncomfortably tight, but it would work.

No sooner had she clicked the last piece in place than the shuttle lurched right hard.

"Hey, what's with the driving?" Ash said.

"It's not me," Kett snarled.

Ash spun to talk to Del again, but the shuttle's thrusters hit hard, plastering her face against the seat. She managed to say, "Hold on," but it probably sounded funny with her mouth pressed sideways. She couldn't breathe. Couldn't talk. The only sound she could hear was the pounding of her heart.

Seconds burned like hours. Black halos closed in on Ash's vision.

Palak whooped. Was she enjoying this?

Ash turned her head enough to look for Tobin, but he must have been in a seat she couldn't see. Maybe closer to the cargo area. Lace wore a calm expression betrayed only by the white-knuckled grip on her seat cushions.

"I'm sorry for dragging you into this," Ash said through gritted teeth.

Lace said, "It's better than rotting in quarantine."

The burn ended and Ash gasped. Her hair floated in front of her face as they dropped into a zero-G drift. The shuttle fine-tuned its direction, making her hair dance oddly in front of her face.

"How's it going up there, Kett?" she asked.

"I'm doing nothing. I have nothing to do to drive this."

"Are the lights on your dashboard mostly blue or mostly red?" Ash said.

"They are almost entirely red."

"That doesn't sound good."

"It's not good," Kett grumbled. "It's not good at all."

Fumbling with her harness, Ash said, "Where's Tobin?"

Lace didn't move, but Del unbuckled herself and drifted back. "He's back in cargo." Then, "Oh no."

"What?" Ash really couldn't get the buckles to

unbuckle. She mashed the button as hard as she could, cracking one of her fingernails.

"The red lights are flashing now," said Kett. "Three that were blue before are now orange."

The lateral thrusters fired again, and the shuttle gently drifted to the right. Ash's stomach made an attempt to exit via her throat. She swallowed it back, blinked hard, and twisted furiously at her buckles.

Palak reached around from behind and unbuckled the clasp. The whole harness fell away. "Get back here," she said.

Ash launched herself up out of her seat, slamming hard into the ceiling. She caught a terrified look from Lace before righting herself.

Kett shouted, "I don't know what it's telling me!"

"Lace," Ash said. "Get up front and help."

The big woman moved without a word.

Ash pushed herself back toward the passage to the cargo area. Del blocked the entrance, but Ash had enough momentum to bowl past.

Much of the cargo had come unbound during the burn. Boxes and biopacks floated lazily through open space, twisting and leaking their contents into the cabin.

"Crap," said Ash. "We need to get this tied down."

A row of red marbles floated by that didn't look like material from an unsecured biopack. At first, the little series of orbs confused her.

Blood.

She brushed aside the debris to get a better look. Tobin floated among it all, one more piece of debris in a cluttered mess of a launch. Ash flailed. She'd lost her grip on the wall. She swore. That didn't help either. Finally, she grabbed a box as it drifted by and shoved off of it, propelling herself toward Tobin.

Tobin was unconscious, drifting in a mass of blood.

"Help me keep him stable," she said, dabbing at the blood with a cloth while absolutely failing to keep herself stable. "Moving in zero-G is impossible," she muttered. But his wound looked less severe with the blood cleared away.

"There's going to be a second burn," Lace said. "We're not in the proper orbit yet."

"How do you know?" asked Ash. "What happens if we skip the second burn?"

Lace said, "Orbit will decay. We'll land somewhere. Hard."

Together, they pulled the scientist out of the cargo hold, dropping him in one of the rearmost seats. They steadied his neck, buckled him down as tightly as they could, and bandaged a cut below his ear. While Ash and Del secured Tobin, Lace made her way to the cockpit.

Lace said. "We have to jettison."

"We can't," Ash gasped.

"It's sloshing around back there," Lace said. "If we don't tie it down in the next thirty seconds it'll throw off our course."

"How do you know?!"

"I'm just reading it!" Lace waved at the screen in front of Kett. "It's right there!"

Ash looked at the central console. She recognized

one of every hundred symbols on the red, blinking screen. Whatever it was saying looked very urgent. She said, "Can we delay that burn?"

"No!" both Kett and Lace said.

"Slow it, then?"

Kett said, "No," but Lace narrowed her eyes and peered at the screen.

"He has a head injury," Ash said. "Maybe something with his spine. We can't risk another full burn."

Lace swiped the screen and brought up a display of changing orbits.

"Twenty seconds till burn," Kett said. "I can read that much."

"How do you get this job without being able to read?" Lace growled.

"Hector and Simon were supposed to do this. They can drive anything." Kett actually sounded impressed. "I'm backup."

"Simon was our translator," Ash said, swallowing a lump of panic in her throat.

"Sounds like all your talent stayed home."

"Ten seconds," Kett said. "Ash, buckle in."

"Got it!" Lace said. "We can do a light burn for longer to put us on a later intercept."

"How much later?" Ash asked.

"Yes or no?" Lace said.

Kett gave a shake of his head. Ash looked back at Tobin, who still lay unconscious strapped into his seat. Blood beaded through the cloth on his forehead. Del had strapped herself in next to him and Palak sat across from her with a terrified expression on her face.

"Do it," Ash said and launched herself back to the nearest seat.

Before she could properly harness herself in, Lace pressed a button on the console and the sequence fired. The door to the cargo section slammed shut. Lateral thrusters fired several times in quick sequence.

"That's it," Kett said. "Our mission will fail."

"Here it goes," Lace said.

Ash clicked her harness in place, and the burn started in earnest. Gentle pressure locked her in place. Stronger than the gravity on planet, but nothing like the breath-stealing giant of their first burn. After a minute, she settled in and calmed herself with long, slow breaths.

She was in space! The realization of it hit her slowly at first, then all at once. Nothing had gone well. The plan was all chaos and uncertainty, but they were in space. She'd made it as far as anyone ever expected. The only other trip through zero-G she had been on had been her trip down to Edge all those years ago. This, launching back up in the shuttle, had been beyond all her dreams. The trip down was supposed to be one way. It always *had* been one way for reasons Ash had never quite understood.

And after she was done, there'd be no chance of ever returning. This was it, her last trip into the great beyond. She would have to make the most of the journey and enjoy it all she could.

The burn finished, and she felt herself drifting in weightlessness again.

"How long?" Ash whispered, almost to herself.

"Too long," said Kett.

Lace's fingers played across the screen for what seemed like an eternity. "Five days."

The words hit Ash like a brick. Five days? "Well, we have supplies for it, I guess," she breathed.

Kett said. "We jettisoned half our cargo."

Ash's heart pounded in her chest. She needed the suits and the tech. What would she do without Hector or Simon? They needed food and water to survive the next five days. Five days! It was supposed to be less than five hours. She did her best to keep her voice from betraying her fear, but probably failed terribly. "What did we lose?"

"I don't know," said Kett, "but we have time to find out and come up with a new plan."

Ash smoothed the front of her coveralls, drew a deep long breath, and prepared herself for the most focused and intense five days of planning she had ever experienced.

CHAPTER SIX

"I THINK I would make a pretty good unreliable narrator," Ash said after an eternity adrift. She floated upside-down in the shuttle, her tablet drifting in front of her face.

"Shouldn't you be helping?" asked Del. "Or putting together a new plan?"

"I'm reading a book about a guy who starts a club where they all punch each other, and then they don't talk about it."

"That sounds... terrible."

Ash spun her tablet around and watched as it floated away. "It's reminiscent of its era."

Del caught the device and attached it to the wall. "You should be focusing on our plan."

Tobin held a data spike up for everyone to see. "We don't need a plan. We have the solution the council approved."

"Can't talk about the plan right now," said Ash.

Del narrowed her eyes. "Why not?"

Ash nodded at the panel array in the back of the shuttle. "Detector still says there's a comm active. Until we find that, we shouldn't talk about anything important at all."

Tobin's expression scrunched up under his fresh bandages. It turned out he'd had zero damage to his spinal cord and his concussion had been mild. "And you're reading instead of helping find it?"

Ash pushed herself toward Tobin and crashed into the seat next to him. "They also make soap in this book. I don't know why."

"So, your tablet survived takeoff, but not the food?" Tobin sounded grumpy for some reason.

Ash said, "Kett is sorting through the remaining supplies."

"It's been almost a day," said Tobin.

Ash spun herself around so she could look Tobin right in the eyes. She guided herself into the seat in front of him, leaned over the back, and met his gaze. "It's a good book."

———

ASH FED the final biopack into the printer. After two days, she was hungry enough to start eating the seat cushions, but it turned out they weren't edible. The printer extruded basic nutrient sludge, which she divided up among the team.

"This is the last of it," she said. "Unless we start recycling our clothes, we're all out of food."

"Our clothes won't recycle into food," said Tobin.

"Except for Kett's shirt, possibly. It's made of plant fibers."

"I don't need anything to eat," said Kett.

"Of course, you do, big guy," said Del. "You probably need more calories than the lot of us combined."

Kett shook his head. "My people can go weeks without food and very little water."

Ash scratched her chin. "Are you fireproof?"

"Resistant," Kett said.

"What if we dunked you in acid?"

"How strong?"

"Quite."

"I would probably be fine."

"How about if we kept you submerged for a really long time?"

"Ash," said Del.

Ash raised an eyebrow.

"I can hold my breath," said Kett. "But it depends on how strong the acid is."

Del swallowed her share of nutrient sludge. "How about you come up with a plan that doesn't get Kett killed?"

Tobin, from the other end of the shuttle, said, "You can talk now."

Ash furrowed her brow. "What?"

Tobin gestured at the console. "There's no comm signal detected."

Ash floated to his end and peered at the device. "But what was it?"

"An error?" Tobin said. "Maybe something was coordinating with the ship, but it stopped."

"Or maybe now it's recording, silently listening to everything we say so that it can report back to its robot overlord while we sleep." Ash peered at the screen. "How can we plan anything if it might be listening?"

Lace floated over from the pilot's cabin. "Problem?"

"We're worried about spies," Ash said. "Last thing we need is a heartless machine listening to our brilliant and elaborate plans."

"Smash and grab is neither of those things," said Tobin.

"I wouldn't call it heartless," said Lace.

Ash said, "It's a merciless ark of death and destruction, seated like an ancient evil god at the center of an eternal starship."

"It brought life to a dead planet," said Lace. "Don't forget that."

"Then killed that life," said Ash. "It's like Pandora unleashing hope on humanity just because that makes all the other plagues so much worse."

Lace's brow wrinkled. "I don't think that's how the story goes."

"Her curiosity and persistence cursed all of humanity forever," Ash peered out the window at the endless stars. "She was a monster."

"Agree to disagree," said Lace. "But I'm not a spy for the machine."

Tobin folded his arms and drifted sideways. "Nobody said it was you."

"Seems to me you'd be pretty stupid not to suspect me."

"We trust you," said Ash. "Completely."

"Maybe it would help if we knew more about you," said Tobin. "Why did you agree to Ash's mission?"

Lace fixed him with a flat look. After a few long breaths, she said, "The world is never big enough for someone like me. Even as an engineer with access to all the hidden corners of the ship, I was a lion circling my cage. I paced long enough to wear holes in the floor." She stared off into the distance. "Then I started to hate the thing that kept me there."

"Traverse," Ash said.

"It told us that you were planning something. Not you, specifically, but that the odds of something were high. It wanted us to send any information we found. We were going to be the moles in your little operation, as if anyone would trust us with critical information." Lace looked around at each of them. "I suppose it wasn't far off. Only, I have no interest in playing by Traverse's rules. Never again."

Ash recognized the vehemence in those last words. "It killed someone you cared about."

"Worse. When I was young, I was in love with a beautiful woman named Talia. She was everything to me, but that wasn't convenient for the machine. I never found out what happened to her, but Traverse made her disappear completely as if she never existed." Her voice was thick with emotion. "I never saw her again, and I poured everything into gaining the skills it took to delve into Traverse's systems, which I think is exactly what Traverse wanted. I had the skills it needed and over the years my memory of Talia faded. The bitterness just—seeps out of you."

Tobin said, "It did what it needed to shape you into what it wanted."

"Exactly," Lace said. She turned and drifted away. "Exactly."

Later, Tobin whispered in Ash's ear. "You can't possibly trust her."

Ash took one of his hands and squeezed it. "We can't afford to not trust anyone, Tobin. If even one person betrays us, this entire heist is sunk. We're all in on this mission. One hundred percent. No holding back."

After a brief pause, Kett spoke from the cargo area, "What are you saying over there?"

"We need your shirt, Kett," Ash said, finally. "We're going to eat it."

———

SOMEONE HAD TAMPERED with the comm detector, and a scan using Ash's multitool showed her the microscopic evidence of the buffered modification. This damage couldn't happen on its own. On the first day of their trip, the device had worked without a problem.

Now, three days into their five-day journey, it was broken.

Ash scoured the cargo hold and double checked Kett's inventory. The weapons were gone except for those carried in the passenger cabin. Palak's spear, Del's pistol, and Tobin's stunner. Nothing remained of their chemical or biological feedstocks. The printer remained but was all but useless without anything to feed it. They had packed cutting tools and breaching equipment in case they ended up needing to punch through the hull of the ship to travel between boroughs. It was a backup plan, but all of that was gone.

But how? She had instructed the team to tie everything down.

Only one of Tobin's fancy suits remained. She tried the invisibility suit on so that she could get the feel for it. The limbs used a mechanical assist, which helped in gravity and caused trouble navigating the zero-G space. The helmet folded back to rest on her shoulders when not in use, and the outside of the suit contained dozens of pockets. The suit's most important feature, however, was the odd black-and-white pattern. More than merely stylish, it was designed to fool Traverse into thinking she was a Skyling. Even though the patterns looked nothing like the modified humans to her, the AI would avoid detecting her if at all possible.

This was her invisibility suit, and now they were left with only one of them. It wasn't enough.

Ash inspected a slashed section of shelving. The ultralight fiber looked melted in a downward arc. Looking back behind that damage, she found a stray cord dangling loose from a loop on the wall. All the others must have flown free during the jettison. Lace's jettison.

She shook the idea from her head. How could she accuse Lace? The loose ends of the cord waved under the gentle tug of her breath. It was a clean cut, with the fibrous ends of the cable fused with heat. Her mother's blue knife could have made these cuts. Did it end up getting jettisoned as well?

Either way, they definitely had a traitor. It could have been anyone on the team.

Ash couldn't trust anyone.

———

ON THE FOURTH DAY, Ash turned to Kett. "How long can you survive in a vacuum?"

"I don't know."

"We have an airlock," Ash said, glancing at the back of the shuttle.

"Ash," said Del. "Stop it."

"I'm bored!"

"Then tell Palak to punch you again."

"No," said Palak.

"Is she always like this?" asked Lace.

"Pretty much," said Tobin. "She usually talks more."

Ash crossed her arms and legs and drifting at a ninety-degree angle. "We're almost over Edge."

Tobin's expression softened. "It'll be like all the other times."

"I know," said Ash. "But I want to look anyway."

When their transit took them over the colony, she brought up their view of the rocky planet on the screen. Plumes of smoke and ash rose from the little spec on the mountain, completely obscuring any assessment they might make of the damage done to the colony. It had been like this for four days, and there were no signs of wind carrying the obscurement away.

And Hector was down there somewhere. She had selfishly wanted to keep him close so that she could keep him safe. Irrational, yes, but it was all she knew. Now, she had no way of knowing how bad the attack was, and she had no way of knowing how Hector had fared.

"How long until the storm hits?" Ash asked. "Maybe that'll clear the atmosphere."

"Months," said Tobin. "For all we know there might be nothing left of Edge."

One quick comm ping to the surface would confirm survivors. It would also reveal their status to Traverse.

"Maybe Traverse would let us off with a warning," said Ash.

Tobin rested a hand on her shoulder. "I'm sorry, Ash. I wish things had gone better too."

"This doesn't mean we're going to switch to your plan."

"There might not be an Edge to return to."

Ash looked up at him. "Do you ever wonder if Traverse is a person?"

"No," said Palak from across the shuttle.

A hint of a smile crossed Tobin's lips. "We debated that for years in the last days of Pyramid, trying to figure out if it was murder to destroy that machine."

Palak floated over, catching herself on the back of a crash seat. "There's no debate. Traverse is a computer."

"What did you come up with?" Ash asked Tobin.

"That anything made isn't alive," Tobin said.

"Exactly," said Palak.

"That's ridiculous," said Ash. "I'm a biologist. I make life all the time."

Lace said, "I thought you assembled dead bits of already-existing things and zapped them to bring them to life. Isn't that how you explained it?"

"There's DNA math involved," Ash said. "It's complicated."

"You said it involved maniacal laughter," said Lace.

"It doesn't matter," Palak growled. "The computer is programmed by a person. It's not a person. How is this hard?"

"That makes sense to me," said Kett.

Too loud, Ash said, "Traverse is not a programmed thing. It's a machine trained and grown like any living thing."

"True," said Tobin. "But it learns the way someone programmed it to learn."

"The architects aren't gods," said Palak.

"They're not?" asked Lace, a mocking smile pulling at the corners of her lips.

"Yeah, it's not like they're biologists," said Ash.

Kett frowned but held his tongue.

"Maybe you should ask it when you get to the core," said Tobin. "How were you planning on doing that, again?"

The shuttle floated in silence for several long breaths before Del added, "It doesn't matter. If it needs to be destroyed, then we do it. We can debate afterward whether or not it was murder."

———

"WHY ALL THIS?" Lace asked. "I thought you were a scientist."

Ash kept her attention on the screen in front of her. It contained a complex diagram of Traverse's override hierarchy. "This is basically science."

Lace pursed her lips. "Is it, though?"

"Sure." Ash looked at the other woman and saw the concern there. "Look, a heist is an experiment. You come up with a wild hypothesis, design a way to test it, and in the end, you record all your results and publish a peer-reviewed paper."

"That—isn't how it works at all."

"Basically, though."

Lace ground her teeth. "I'm starting to regret this."

"It's only been four days!"

"We've been out of food for two, and Kett's shirt wasn't exactly nutrient dense."

Ash swiped her diagram and adjusted the view. She saw the dependency lines that connected each instance to the one in the core, but she couldn't find a way to map each instance to a borough. "We're going to need to download a map once we're on the ship unless you know how to directly access the core."

Lace let out a long sigh. "I've already told you. I can get you to the elevator, but any attempt to open it without authorization is going to trigger a vote."

"And all the other peer instances will see something's wrong." She spun the diagram. "What if we control every other voting instance?"

"What kind of science do you do, Ash?"

"The good kind."

"You know the feeling you get when you've hit on the discovery that will change everything?"

Ash thought to her ideas about the homeostasis equation. She could change Sky forever if that could ever be tested and implemented. She kept her mouth shut.

"This isn't that," drawled Lace. "Even if you can spike one instance and convince it to open the doors, the other adjacent instances will immediately deploy corrections."

"Just the adjacent ones?" Ash asked.

"You need them all," said Lace. "It's not possible."

THE STARSHIP TRAVERSE had traveled three hundred years from planet Earth and settled into its orbit around Sky over a thousand years ago. Ash had lived her young life aboard the ship in one of its boroughs—the city-within-a-city that constituted one micro-environment for the development of talent to use in the colony below. She had read about how the ship functioned and how its pieces fit together. In her long days planning for the heist, Ash had gathered as much information as she could on Traverse. She knew the ship was big.

Nothing prepared her for what she saw.

Traverse hung in the void against the backdrop of Sky. It was a loose-knit cylinder of interconnected nodes. Hundreds of them. Through the weave of the rotating mass, she could see the inner sphere of the core. An interface layer spun with the center of the ship, connected to each borough via a single long cylinder.

"Autopilot has engaged," Lace said. "The shuttle is steering us back to its borough."

"Is it a good one?" Ash asked.

"It's roughly in the middle, and as far as I know it's as good as any."

Ash watched the starship through their window for a long time, silently counting the nodes as they rotated around the core. "Huh," she said.

"What?" Lace asked.

"I thought it would be an odd number based on the design documents."

Tobin drifted by waggling his data spike. "Do you have your plan figured out yet?"

"I'm working on it."

She wasn't working on it. Not even a little.

———

"ASH," Del whispered after yet another pass over the planet, "we don't know if there's an Edge anymore."

"It doesn't matter."

"It *does*." Del ran fingers through her stubby hair. The days without food had made her pale and lean as if the stocky woman needed any help looking meaner. "If we're going to die anyway, then killing Traverse isn't self-defense."

"You mean destroying Traverse?"

"It means that what we call it matters. And what we do to the humans up there matters."

Ash blinked slowly. "We don't have a choice."

Del shook her head. "We could each find our way into a borough. Live out our lives there."

"Give in," Ash whispered. "Forever." Ash spun her multitool around in front of her face, catching and spinning it again, over and over. Del might be right. Maybe they could make a life up here. Ash wanted desperately to talk to Hector about the ideas bouncing around in her head. He was always so good at parsing right from wrong.

She choked back thoughts of Hector. That final image of him with Simon, ducking into the trench to brave the meteor storm. Would that be the last she ever saw of him? Five days had already passed. Either he was dead or he'd wait patiently. She forced herself to slow down and think.

"I have a new plan, and it's going to take some patience." When she saw the skeptical expressions on their faces, she added, "Yes, I'm capable of being patient."

CHAPTER SEVEN

"I HATE THIS," Ash said in the dark elevator. This is taking too long."

Kett grumbled, "Do you always whine so much when you're sneaking?"

"If I open the helmet of my invisibility suit, the doors will detect me, and it'll let us out." The suit's powered joints clicked as she bounced with nervous energy. The black-and-white pattern covering the suit didn't resemble Kett or the Seasiders at all, but so far Traverse's automated systems had completely ignored her.

Ash hated being invisible. They were alone in the dark elevator that had taken them up from the shuttle's docking bay. Next to her stood a mean-looking spider sentry robot the size of a horse, and for some reason, the doors hadn't opened yet to give it access to the city.

It had probably been days.

"It's been ten minutes," said Kett. "This happens."

"Is this what it's like for you living in Edge?" Ash asked. "This is horrible."

"It's not so bad. Usually, we pry open doors if they will not open automatically."

"You have to open doors yourself?" Ash felt her way along the elevator doors. "Maybe we can force these doors open."

"Be patient," said Kett. "It's not worth the risk."

"I'll open my helmet."

"If you remove your invisibility suit, you'll alert Traverse to our presence." He tapped on the bladed front pincers of the security spider.

A blinking light in her helmet told Ash that she was using too much oxygen, alerting her to the fact that she was panic-breathing. "But we could run away."

Kett shrugged. "Traverse thinks you're dead."

"We could starve," Ash said.

"I don't have any more shirts." He wasn't wearing a shirt. He had refused, even after they'd found some perfectly adequate feedstock for their printer.

The door whooshed open, and burning yellow light cut through Ash's clear helmet to drive a spike directly into her headache. She took a single step forward before Kett bowled her out of the way, landing them both in a heap outside the elevator. The spider thumped past, seemingly unaware of their passage.

"Robots won't pause for you when you wear this suit," said Kett.

The skyline curved up and away, tracing the inside arc of the borough's node. Buildings and garden plots dotted the lower reaches. Light bloomed in the sky like the yellow sun of Earth, and far off, near the horizon, the larger buildings of business and tech districts loomed. She rushed down the street and looked the other way, something clicking into place in her heart. She had longed for this place. The science district lined that opposite wall, its tall buildings cantilevered out against the northernmost wall.

This wasn't her home borough, but it was home. This was the place she'd left so long ago to work on the colony of Edge. Left to never return.

Yet here she was.

Home.

It was a strange version of home, with colors slightly off due to the yellow sun and signs written in a strange pictogram language. She even recognized store-fronts from her home and marveled at the way logos changed with the strange language.

Voices brought Ash from her reverie. There were others nearby, because of course there were. This was a city in the sky. It couldn't exist without people.

She took Kett's elbow and quietly led him down an alley.

"Did they see you?" Kett whispered.

"I'm way too sneaky," said Ash. "We need to get to this borough's central park. That's where Lace says the main terminal will be."

Kett climbed atop a short building and peered out at the city. With some effort, he helped Ash up onto the roof. "We can cross atop these buildings without being seen, then drop down a short distance from the park."

Ash opened her mouth to protest, but the big man

took three big strides and leaped to the next building. She watched as he continued, bounding from one structure to the next.

She flexed her muscles and hopped on the balls of her feet. Her invisibility suit had a slight mechanical assist, to help her with tasks that might be beyond her physically. She didn't know if it would let her jump like Kett.

Below, she heard the voices again. Peering down, she saw several men and women dressed in the outfits of twenty-first-century Earth. The long sleek lines of their formalwear blended nicely with the elegant curves of their bodies. There were ten of them, and they laughed like drunken revelers.

Ash drew a deep breath, ran, and jumped.

The air rushed past, and she hit the next building near the center. As she dropped to one knee, her gloved fingers slammed into the black roof, sending a spray of grit into the air.

"That was amazing," she whispered to herself.

Six buildings away, Kett jumped again. He slammed into the side of a taller building and scaled it, hardly breaking pace.

Ash gave a whoop and ran after him, leaping from building to building, slowing only to reassess her bearings. They ran straight for the center of the borough, adjusting only for the angle of the curving streets.

When she reached the taller buildings, she didn't slow. She relied on the clawed fingertips of her suit and the muscular assist that allowed her to leap so high.

She hit the wall hard, knocking the breath out of

her lungs. A crack spiderwebbed across her helmet, and only two fingers found purchase in the fibrous simulated stone of the taller building. Ash hung for a dozen shattering heartbeats. Below, pedestrians walked as if nothing had happened, no doubt enjoying the mundane dullness of their regular lives. Above, high enough that she would suffer serious injury from the drop, Ash hung by her aching fingertips. The oxygen warning light in her suit flashed red for her excessive consumption.

Ash scrabbled at the wall. How had Kett found such good purchase? There were no good handholds. She scraped at the wall with the claws of her loose hand, swearing as the tips broke against the hard fiber.

Anyone looking up would see her. Traverse might not be able to process her existence while in the suit, but if enough people reacted to her, it would certainly notice that.

Her grip slipped. A crumble of the fibrous wall fell like dust across her glass-fronted helmet. Muscles ached. The mechanical assist wasn't designed for this angle, so her own body had to do the work.

There! Ash spotted the holes where Kett had dug his claws into the wall. She smashed her own fingertips into the handhold and, with tremendous, aching effort, pulled herself up.

Again, and again, she found Kett's claw marks. When she finally deposited herself in a heap atop the roof, her arms and back ached, and she didn't think she would ever move again.

"I see it," said Kett from the other side of the roof. "In the center of the garden."

Ash crawled over and sat next to him. Below, a forest of aspen and willow waved gently in a manufactured breeze. People walked through the park along paved paths, hand in hand or alone. In the center of the green space, nestled in an oak grove, sat a small utility shed.

"Are you ready?" asked Kett.

"Not really," she gasped. She leaned back against the short perimeter wall and held her helmet in her hands. "I'm sorry about all this, Kett."

He sat next to her. "They say you aren't capable of apologies."

"They're mostly right, but I don't understand why you don't care about Traverse. It won't open doors for your people or feed you from the food printers. You'll struggle forever if we don't do anything."

Kett stared up at the orange glow of the fading sun. "We get food from other people and from the earth, just as we always have. We open our own doors. Our culture is born of struggle and removing that puts my people in as much risk."

"Or it could save them from oppression."

A rumble rolled deep in Kett's chest. "Is Edge the same since the people of Pyramid came? Is there anything left of what it once was?"

Ash thought back to the days when Edge was a tiny science outpost. Those had been wonderful times, but now the city of Edge offered wonders she never expected. "It's different," she said finally, "but it isn't exactly what the Pyramidians want. It's like the city has combined the wills of its various people and become something else entirely. Unpredictable, almost, but with a personality all its own."

"You make it sound like an artificial intelligence."

Before Ash could respond, the sun faded from orange to the deep blue of night. Above, the false sun turned silvery white, blanketing the city in shadow. The hairs on the back of her neck stood on end, and for a moment she felt as though she were being watched. Ash peered out over the rooftops but saw nothing. The pedestrian traffic below slowed to a trickle.

On an alley-facing side of the building sat a metal staircase that creaked like rusty gears when Ash stepped on it.

"You know, these buildings can't even burn. This fire escape is just here because they had them on Earth, and the architects wanted as many similarities with home as possible."

"Did they burn their buildings a lot?"

"Constantly."

With the cover of darkness, Ash and Kett had no trouble navigating the park without being seen. They made their way through the rustling trees, past grassy fields and neatly bundled patches of wildflowers. Ash had forgotten how beautiful the ship was and had to force herself to keep going rather than revel in the memories she had of her own borough. The layout was exactly the same, and the subtle differences were invisible under the light of the false moon.

Ash stopped. Leaves rustled nearby in the darkness. She peered into the small forest, trying to make out movement in the shadows.

Nothing.

The utility shed stood ten feet square with a ceramic roof and small, blacked-out windows. The only hints that it might contain more than gardening supplies were the advanced digital lock and odd lightning bolt pictograph on the door. Ash connected her tablet to the lock, and despite the shattered screen, managed to navigate menus until she found the override. Within minutes, she had the door open.

The inside of the building stood in shocking contrast to the park outside. Slick black machines choked the space, and under the floor grate, the machinery descended into the blackness like the throat of a starving monster. Thick black tentacles, not unlike the technology of Pyramid, coiled around a console in one corner.

Ash connected her tablet to the wiring and navigated the programs. Biographical information on each member of her team flashed across the broken display before loading into Traverse's central system.

"I can do minor updates like this," Ash said, "which will affect only this borough's instance of Traverse. It'll now recognize us as members of this community."

Kett grunted his response. "And then we'll have access."

"If I try to give us any special authority—like promoting us to be engineers or architects—it'll trigger a vote. The five adjacent instances of Traverse will weigh in, and we'll all be overridden." When Kett didn't respond, she amended, "Overridden means murdered."

"Wonderful."

Ash swiped through the menus again and located Tobin's program. This was the one he wanted to use to destroy Traverse from the inside. It would corrupt all systems and cause a catastrophic cascade of destruction throughout the ancient ship's systems. Her finger hovered over the engage sequence. This could all be finished. Submitting immediately would end every-thing—at a cost.

But what else could she do? Anything else was risking failure, and for the first time in her life, she suspected that failure might be a distinct possibility. Maybe even *likely*. She closed her eyes and drew a deep breath to steady herself.

She desperately wanted to get back to Edge and see how Hector fared in the attack. The image of him in those last seconds, dazed and bleeding, flashed again on the backs of her eyelids. In her mind, the potential damage grew worse with every passing day. What if Edge was destroyed in the meteor attack? What if Hector needed medical attention?

With a few quick strokes, she set the tablet's timer. She left it connected and stuffed it back behind the mess of computing equipment.

"Done," she said, stepping out of the shed. She pulled her helmet back and grinned at Kett. "Records are updated, and our teammates are now official residents of this borough." The scent of fresh earth growing plants settled the unease in her soul. "Welcome home."

CHAPTER EIGHT

"I LOVE DESIGNING EXPERIMENTS," Ash said. "It's just a lot of work actually doing them."

Over the past week, she had made many friends, but her favorite was Rossi, the scientist who walked with her every day to and from the science district. By chance, she studied biology, and Ash reveled in the ability to talk shop with another very smart woman.

"But what is your hypothesis?" asked Rossi, a woman of slight build and reddish-brown skin. "And how would you test it?"

"Think of DNA as a kind of advanced math," Ash said. They rounded a corner and Ash almost succeeded in her attempt to not glance at the rooftops. A flicker of movement danced away as she did, and her train of thought sputtered to a halt. "It's very complicated."

Rossi laughed. "Of course, it's complicated. That's why biology is the best science."

Rossi was the best.

Standing halfway up the block in front of a cheery

yellow teahouse, Kett, in his ragged indigo pants, no shirt, and dark sunglasses, looked like a bad omen.

Ash gestured with a sweep of her arm at Kett. The silky wrap she wore felt like an ocean of fabric. "This is my stop. Have you met my friend Kett?"

Rossi didn't so much as glance at the big man. "It's been lovely, Ash. Same time tomorrow morning?"

"I'll let you know," said Ash. She hugged Rossi and watched as she left.

"Everyone else is inside," said Kett as he pulled the door open.

The Hibiscus Teahouse was a version of a place Ash used to go with her mother. Aromas of sandalwood and rose suffused the false wood building, and plants hung like clouds from high rafters. Ash made her way through the maze of dividers to a secluded table where her team already waited. Tobin had disabled Traverse's surveillance of this one large booth, and they had met there every day since they'd arrived.

Ash pushed her way onto the bench seat, and Kett did the same across from her, eliciting grumbles from Tobin and Del, who also shared the big man's side. Ash, Palak, and Lace had no trouble fitting on their side, but Ash didn't point that out.

"What have we learned?" Ash asked.

Lace said, "My engineering creds are still valid. I can get you to the recycler level, but I still can't get you to the core."

Palak, whose spear sat awkwardly between her and Lace, said, "Our shadow still eludes me. She knows secret passages through the city." They had all noticed someone following them throughout the week. Only Palak had come close enough to see the girl in the white dress.

A server came to the table with cups and tea. The team waited in silence as he placed thin ceramic mugs down one at a time and poured steaming hot tea. When he left, Kett was the only one without a drink.

"I'm not thirsty anyway," he said.

Ash took a sip of her hibiscus tea. It was sweet and warm and reminded her of the time her mother told her that there was more to life than science grades and old movies. She had been wrong, of course. "Are you sure?" she asked Kett.

Kett said, "We located four of the five passages connecting this borough to the adjacent ones. He glanced at Del. "They are all guarded by spider sentries. Only three of them are guarded by people."

Del's hand drifted to the energy pistol at her belt. It was the key to their whole plan, along with Palak's spear, and Ash wondered at what was going through her mind.

"Tobin?" Ash said, turning to the man.

The scientist placed five comm units on the table. "Modified and updated. We should be able to use Lace's wireless network keys to locate each other and communicate."

"Safely?"

He sighed. "There are so many layers of surveillance. I scraped away as much as I could."

"So, emergencies only." It wasn't ideal, but it would give them a way to coordinate timing once the plan was in motion. "We'll just have to speak in double-secret encryption."

"Traverse would know."

"I think if we speak in Navajo we should be fine," said Ash.

"What is Navajo?" asked Kett.

Ash had no idea. "It's complicated."

The server stepped up to their table and stood quietly. He blinked rapidly several times, smiled, and said, "Can I get you anything else?"

Ash exchanged a look with Tobin that reassured her that the server's behavior was indeed odd. "Yes," she said waving a hand loosely in Kett's direction. "My friend here didn't get any tea."

The server took two steps back. He blinked rapidly again several times.

"That'll be fine," Tobin said. "We don't need anything else." When the server left, he leaned forward and whispered, "We can't keep meeting like this. There is something very wrong with the people here, and the more we meet as a group, the more we're stressing them."

"They'll be fine," whispered Ash. "A little stress is good for people."

Tobin growled, "It's not them I'm worried about."

"But the people here are so nice," Ash said. She turned to Lace. "You know something about this."

The big woman swallowed the rest of her tea. "We should leave."

One by one, they left the teahouse. If Traverse watched closely, it would know they had been together, but Ash suspected the AI of this borough had more interesting things to focus on. The place was a pleasant, bustling city by day and a vibrant, exciting place at night. What would it want with six insignificant residents?

Kett left first, followed quickly by Tobin and Lace. Palak went out the back a few minutes later, leaving Del looking exhausted and alone in the corner of her booth.

"It's getting to him, you know," Del grumbled.

"Kett?" Ash slid so that she sat across from Del. "He told me he's fine."

"He's invisible here."

"He was invisible back in Edge."

Del shook her head. "Something's happening here that makes people pretend not to see him."

"I don't understand why they would go along with this."

Del shook her head. "It hurts him, being ignored like that. Every time."

"We're almost ready."

"You're *not*. You heard Lace. She's still not going to let you get to the core. Either she doesn't know or she's not going to spill."

"I just need to gain her trust," said Ash, failing to quell the uncertainty in her voice.

Del drew a long deep breath and said, "I'm leaving."

"Yeah, you can go first," glancing at the teahouse entrance. A slender figure stood by the door in a white dress.

Del didn't move. "No, Ash. You don't need me anymore. Not with whatever plan you have here. I'm taking that open passage to the next borough, and you won't see me again."

Ash blinked at Del several times, willing the words to form that would convince the older woman to stay. None presented themselves, so she said, "I think it's the shadow. By the door."

Del's lips pressed together in a tight line. With almost no movement she cast a glance at the girl in the white dress. "Give me a count of sixty." She set her tea down and made her way toward the back exit.

Around thirty-five, Ash stole another glance at the girl. Her gaze met the pale blue of the teenage girl's eyes and held them for almost two whole seconds.

The girl ran.

Ash leaped up from the booth, spilling the remains of her tea. The billowy silk of her wrap tangled on the chairs as she passed, upsetting customers, and slowing her down. By the time she got to the door, the girl was nowhere to be seen.

Del rounded the corner. Her shoulders tensed when she saw Ash standing in the street.

"We'll miss you," said Ash.

Del pulled her into a hug. The woman's energy pistol dug into Ash's hip, but it didn't matter. The first of her team was leaving, abandoning the cause, and there was nothing she could do about it.

CHAPTER NINE

THERE WAS a family living in the apartment on the third floor of the building at the corner of Clover and Sixteenth Street, where Ash had grown up with her mother and father. She watched them for hours from across the narrow street, sipping coffee and reading scientific journals on a tablet Rossi had given her. Lace had configured it to translate the pictograph language so that the articles made sense. The focus of every piece veered toward the topic of homeostasis, approaching the challenge from a variety of wrong angles.

The family had a spider plant hanging in their window rather than mums, but Ash could almost imagine her own mother bustling around the place during the day. Her mother had been a brilliant scientist, and *she* had returned to the ship to live her own life. Ash wasn't mad at Del for her decision. How could she be?

Ash glanced down at her tablet, which displayed the empty comment field under a naïve statement by some junior scientist. Her skin itched at the idea of leaving his idiot statement about the impossibility of self-sustaining balance alone, but she didn't have time for a protracted battle in the comments section. Tobin's drop would be soon, and she couldn't afford to miss it.

It proved too dangerous to meet after the teahouse. Whenever two or more of her team approached the same block, residents twitched with stress.

Stress would lead to discovery. Ash still had the slip of paper where Tobin explained it to her. Traverse could detect stress, and it could detect patterns. If it had enough information, it would find them, and Ash didn't like how Traverse tended to solve such problems.

She cast one last glance at the family in the other apartment. They looked happy. The mother helped the young girl with homework. The father punched buttons on a food printer. Ash's father had known how to program the best nutrient cubes.

The street was full of pedestrians rushing home from their jobs in the late afternoon. Ash blended with the crowd, merging seamlessly in her casual wrap and white sneakers. A headband wrangled the wild cacophony of her hair, and she wore glasses printed to resemble classic thick-framed Ray-Bans. From outside, she knew she looked like a hundred other women walking their errands through the bustling city. Traverse, if it tried, would still be able to pick her out with no problem, but at least her presence wouldn't cause stress among the people.

The girl in the white dress had grown sloppy over the few weeks since that last meeting at the teahouse.

Ash spotted her right away, but this time the girl wasn't on the roof of an adjacent building or hiding in the entrance to an alley. Instead, she sat alone on a bench with her hands folded in her lap. Ash used the chaos of a mother herding three children to move closer without being noticed. The girl's mouth pressed into a frown and a tight tension carried between her eyebrows.

Ash sat on the bench. "Please don't run."

The girl tensed but did not move. The pedestrian traffic flowed around them, parting like dust in a strong wind. After a long while, the girl finally spoke. "When will you take that monster and leave?"

Ash's brow furrowed. "Kett? He's not so bad."

The girl cast around. "When?"

"I'm Ash."

For several long breaths, Ash wasn't sure the girl would respond. Then, she whispered, "Ianthe."

Three women passed in business suits. As they walked by, they stared at Ash without blinking. Across the street, a man in a hoodie glanced her way as well. Ash's skin crawled. Something felt very strange about the way they watched her.

And there were others too. Even the children watched her, staring at her as if she might pull a weapon or explode in a shower of fireworks.

"Do you want to walk somewhere?" Ash asked.

"Yeah."

Ash picked a direction and did her best to blend with the other walkers. At first, it was difficult. People still stared at her as if she'd forgotten to wear clothing.

Then, slowly, they lost interest and, with Ianthe trailing shortly behind, she managed to become invisible again.

As they walked, Ianthe spoke. "The people here aren't what they seem. They're just ants, always doing their work and tending their borough. When I was younger, there were more people like me. My parents were like me. Traverse always helped us, and I don't think people really had a problem with it. My grandparents were from Earth, and they were some of the original travelers."

Ash wanted to tell the girl that what she said wasn't possible. The ship had been in orbit around Sky for over a thousand years. Her grandparents couldn't possibly be actual residents of Earth, unless they already possessed the same kind of technology that allowed Tobin to survive in stasis for so long. Her mind wandered on the possibilities of such technology and space travel.

But Ianthe was still talking. "It happened slowly at first. Or, maybe, they were always there, and I figured it out slowly as I grew up. People were no longer people. Not if you really started to get to know them. They went to work, they played games, they watched television. All the things normal people did, but there wasn't anything beyond that." Ianthe swallowed and when she spoke again it was in a carefully steady tone. "My best friend was one of them and I never knew it until it was too late."

They walked in silence for a time. Ash turned toward the park, where she knew she would find

Tobin's drop. Pedestrian traffic thinned, and above, the sun faded to a deep orange.

"We would talk for hours, but one day I discovered that she didn't want anything of her own. She just sort of existed. She played video games and watched the birds. Whenever we talked about our futures, she would make really vague suggestions, and if I showed any interest, she would say that's what she wanted to do, and it was going to be great. I asked her once if she wanted to leave ever, and she just talked about doing whatever was best for the borough or the ship or Traverse."

"Did she ever talk about the planet?"

Ianthe shook her head once. "That's not for a couple hundred years. Nobody thinks about that." Ianthe stopped walking. "What do you want, Ash?"

Ash stopped as well. The flow of traffic parted around them, but she didn't draw attention like she had at the bench. She waited until a gap in the flow so she could speak without someone overhearing. "I want to walk in the void of space, destroy Traverse, and return home in a blaze of glory."

"Is that really what you want?"

"Not really, but it's close enough for now." Ash started walking again. She spotted the package nestled behind a recycler and swiped it up as she passed.

Ianthe followed.

Ash read the card on the tightly wrapped paper bundle. *Programming is complete,* it said in Tobin's messy handwriting. *Sunset tomorrow.*

"How would you like to help me out?" Ash asked. "I have an opening on my team."

Ianthe didn't move. "Before you came, things were fine here. People went about their business. I could study or play or do whatever I wanted."

"Sounds like paradise." Ash continued walking, casting her voice back so that Ianthe could hear. "But you're not happy, are you?"

"I have everything I could possibly want."

"You have what a lot of people have always wanted. Complete freedom to do whatever you want all the time." She considered for a moment. "I could get used to this."

Ianthe walked so silently that Ash had to cast a quick glance behind her to verify that the girl was still there.

"It's not all good, though, is it?"

"I don't think I'm supposed to be here," Ianthe whispered. "When my parents left, I think I was supposed to go with."

Ash turned to the girl. Ianthe had been abandoned by everyone, alone in a borough full of strange people who never engaged her directly. It had to have been a painfully lonely existence. Ash couldn't imagine the pain of that loss. She'd left her parents behind, later to discover that Traverse had killed them both. Ianthe probably hadn't figured out her parents' fate.

"They're dead," Ianthe said. "I figured that much out." The sun faded from orange to its dim blue simulation of a single moon. "Sometimes I wish I had gone with."

"You can come with me if you want, Ianthe."

"Blaze of glory?"

A thrill of excitement ran up Ash's back. Things were finally in motion. She pointed at a nearby building. "We meet in that warehouse at sunset tomorrow." She hesitated. "Kett's going to be there. I hope you don't have a problem working with monsters."

Ianthe's brow furrowed. "The naked man in the park isn't a monster. I talked to him a couple days ago and he's very nice."

"Naked?"

Ianthe's pale skin turned pink. "Mostly."

Ash bit her lip. "Then who's the monster?"

"The woman with the tattoos. She's an engineer, and I don't think she has your best interests in mind."

"Lace?" A mischievous grin spread across Ash's face. "Oh, I know. She's the worst."

"It's not funny. If you're doing what you say, then she's going to betray you. I've seen what her kind can do. They control the machines."

As Ash backed away to fade into the city, she called out, "A heist isn't any fun if there's not a betrayal."

Ash made her way into the park, weaving through paths she now knew well. At the utility shed, she used the wireless adapter on her multitool to update the timer she had set on the tablet. One more day ought to be enough. She took the message card that Tobin had left her and tucked it under a rock at the corner of the shed. Kett would find it there when he looked later that night.

Having finished her tasks, she wandered through

the park. Silver light from above made looming shadows of the trees, and every muted sound felt like a call into the darkness.

The paths had been different in her borough, but she had walked this path with her parents many times as a child. It was part of what had turned her on to biology. After all, if such amazing life could exist in this bottle of a space station, what could they grow on the planet? The aroma of rich soil and living plants had never taken root on the planet, though, and to get there she had given up on her own parents.

They had been retired by Traverse. Killed to conserve resources. A bitter taste burned at the back of Ash's mouth. That thing—that computer—had caused so much pain over the years. So much death. How could she help but hate the thing that ruined so many lives?

How could she not destroy it?

Her thoughts broke when another sound worked its way through the trees. It was a choking sound. Or the croak of a toad. She slowed and very quietly moved off the path toward it.

A pond sat in a small clearing, its still water catching the silver moonlight from above. There, with his back turned to her, sat Kett, his big, hairy shoulders shaking. He wasn't naked, but he wore no shirt and his pants were tattered rags. It took her a moment to realize that he was sobbing. He cupped his face in his hands, but the tears caught the moonlight.

"Kett?" she whispered. "Are you hurt?"

He lowered his hands and steadied himself. "I'm sorry," he said. "You should not have seen that."

She sat next to him on the stone and stared into the pond's inky blackness. There were words that would comfort Kett, but Ash didn't know what they were. "Hang in there. I need you to carry something tomorrow." Those definitely weren't it.

"Why me?"

"Are you afraid?"

Kett looked down at his hands, which were still wet from tears. "I have never been so far from home."

"Not many people have ever been this far from home."

He waved a clawed hand to gesture at the forest. "Look at this place, though. It's paradise. The temperature is perfect. The days are long. There is food everywhere and beauty in everything."

Ash thought of Del and sighed. "Don't tell me you want to give up too."

His eyes grew hard. "I have no purpose here. If I have nothing here, then perhaps I never truly had a purpose back there. I drift."

Ash rested a hand on the big man's shoulder. She wanted to tell him his purpose—the one thing he was going to have to do that nobody else could do. The words hovered at the tip of her tongue, ready to dance free and ruin the most horrible of surprises.

But she couldn't. If Traverse heard, it might ruin their plan.

"You have a purpose," she said, "and that's to carry

things. When that's done, we'll find you a new purpose. I promise."

With that, she left the monster in the woods to spend the night with his own thoughts. There was a very good chance it would be his last.

CHAPTER TEN

EVERYTHING WAS GOING ACCORDING to plan.

The warehouse sat in the center of the tech district, full to the top with the stagnant air of failed industry. Tobin had selected it for its isolated and abandoned nature as well as its location in a seemingly defunct section of the otherwise bustling city. It stood like a bunker on its own block, with high fences surrounding it and inert sentry spiders looming over locked entrances.

Ash wore her invisibility suit over the sleek black of a tactical flight suit. The fabric pulled against her skin when she moved, and the invisibility suit's mechanical enhancements felt good after weeks of impractical—but quite fashionable—trends from the late twenty-first century of Earth. She spotted Ianthe a few blocks from the warehouse and gestured for the girl to follow quietly.

The district wasn't as abandoned as she had hoped, but everything went according to plan. She snuck past a roving band of teens with spiky hair and tight black leathers. Ianthe stopped her before she stepped right in front of a man on the corner selling hotdogs. Going around, the two found the break in the fence that led to the open side entrance.

Ash folded her helmet down and let it rest against her shoulders. Kett and Palak stood next to a large duffel bag, and Lace and Tobin spoke in harsh whispers. Kett showed no signs of the breakdown she had witnessed the night before, but he still only wore a ragged pair of pants. Everything was going according to plan.

Tobin said, "It won't work. Tell her that we need to apply the spike immediately before the override is triggered from above. On my way over, I almost ran into sentry crawlers. Those don't patrol in groups unless Traverse is on a higher alert level."

"You tell her," Lace said, folding her arms.

"She won't listen to me." Tobin saw Ash approaching across the dark warehouse floor. "I'll tell her."

"There's really no need," Ash said. "I won't listen."

Tobin said, "I don't know why the override hasn't triggered yet," proving once again that he was a terrible listener. "But it's close."

"Everything is in place," Ash said. "We'll be in the core by midnight."

Tobin opened his mouth, then closed it again. Maybe he finally understood exactly how wrong he was going to be.

Ash set her pack on the ground. She really did

understand his concerns. If they tried to reach the core and failed, they wouldn't have time to get back to the utility shed. "Your backup plan is in place," she said. "It has been this whole time. The timer is set."

"If the core override is triggered before your timer goes off, the core instance will control every instance across the ship." Tobin's face turned a deep red. "Your timed backup will be pissing into the wind."

Ash gestured at the side door where Ianthe stood wringing her hands. "I'd like you all to meet Ianthe."

Lace's expression darkened. "What's this all about?"

"She's going to help us."

"I don't see how she's much help," Lace said.

"I need you in place, Tobin," Ash gestured for Ianthe to come closer, and the girl approached cautiously. "Your delivery has to be timed just right. Do you have your spike still?"

Tobin withdrew his data spike from an inside pocket. "I am a responsible human being, Ash."

"I'll contact you via the comm when it's time." Ash nodded to the duffel. "You made the gear?"

"Two invisibility suits, as good as those are anymore, but you have the only stunner. I couldn't override the systems to make more weapons." Tobin opened the bag and withdrew one of the suits. "I think I need one suit, and the other can go to someone else."

Palak stepped forward, gripping her spear in one hand. "I don't need one."

"You do," Ash said. "Because you're going with Tobin."

"What?" Tobin snapped. "No, she's not."

"She is." Ash stepped close to Tobin, so she could feel his hot breath. "You'll need the help."

Tobin clenched his jaw so tight his infuriating words were barely audible. "That wasn't the plan."

"You don't know the plan." Ash grabbed a handful of his shirt and pulled him closer. "You've never known the plan, Tobin," she whispered so only he could hear. "Do as I say and don't question it."

Tobin seethed. She thought for a second that he might protest, but instead he pulled himself free and backed up several steps to don his suit. The white and black patterns looked garish under the warehouse's dim light, and Ash couldn't quite see how the random-seeming pattern of lines would evoke an algorithmic detection of a Seasider. Palak, without a word, took the second suit and pulled it over her tight-fitting fatigues.

With the suits gone, the last item in the duffel bag glinted in the dim light. It was a pill-shaped lump of metal the size of a femur, with knobby extrusions on its ends and a slick outer coating.

"Is that the robot?" Ash asked.

"It's as good as it's going to get," said Tobin.

Ash turned to Lace. "And you can still get us to the recycler?"

Lace said, "I can take you there, but it won't do you any good. That robot will be slag before it reaches the interchange."

Ash poked at the robot's slime-coated exterior. "We've coated it in organic material, which the recycling process will have trouble breaking down."

"This won't work," said Lace. "I already told you—"

"People like saying that," Ash snapped, her irritation bubbling dangerously at the surface. "But that's not what I need you for. I need you to tell me you can get us there."

"Organic material won't go to the core recycler. It'll get sorted the other direction."

Ash stared the woman down. Everything was going according to plan.

"Fine," Lace said. "I can get you there."

The walls of the warehouse creaked as if bending under tremendous pressure. Ash looked up at the ceiling, but all she could see was black nothing.

Kett closed the duffel bag with the robot and slung it over his shoulder. "We should go," he said.

While the others prepared, Ash stepped up to Palak and pulled her close. She cast a glance at Tobin. "He's going to try to deploy early," she said.

Palak's grip tightened on her spear. "I don't know if I can do this, Ash."

"Do you need me to draw you a diagram?"

Palak looked around at the others. "You already drew me a diagram, remember? Your penmanship is atrocious."

"Then there's no problem."

Palak's grip tightened on her spear. "I just don't know if I can do it. When I killed Seth, it was easier. I hated him."

"This is nothing like that."

"Isn't it?" She looked around, as the warehouse

made more strange noises. "I can't help but feel like something is wrong with this whole thing."

Ash gripped the woman's hands in her own and gave her one last reassuring nod. Everything was going according to plan.

Palak opened her mouth to talk but was interrupted by a shout from Ianthe.

"It's moving," the girl said, pointing at the big front door.

A boom shook the warehouse. Scratching like claws on concrete resonated through the building.

"This is it," said Tobin. "We shouldn't have gathered. This was all a mistake."

Ash didn't bother to tell him that the gathering had been an absolute necessity. The consequences might be ugly, but there was something she needed to do. She pulled Tobin's data spike from one of her many pockets. "Who's the responsible one now?"

He patted his pockets, his expression changing from horror to rage. "You stole it."

"You can't trust anyone, Tobin," she said, tossing it to him. "That's why we needed to meet. I need to look you in the eyes and tell you that we have a plan. It's a good one, and all it requires is for you to wait."

Tobin's nostrils flared. He crammed the spike in a pocket and sealed it away.

With a crack of thunder and the screech of metal, the door flew wide open and the frame tore in two. A sentry spider from outside crawled down from the outside wall, squeezing its bulk through the newly widened gap. Its red eyes burned with furious energy.

Ash shouted, "Palak, Tobin. Helmets up. Kett, grab the stuff. Lace and Ianthe, you're with Kett and me."

Tobin and Palak sealed their helmets. Palak, spear at her side, crouch walked up alongside the spider. Tobin gave it a wide berth.

"Traverse," Ash called to the spider, walking up to it at a brisk pace. "It's good to see you."

Kett fell in at her side. "What are you doing?"

"She's doing what she always does," Lace said. "Something stupid."

"This is an anomaly," boomed Traverse through the spider. Its crimson eyes focused on Ash. "Explain this gathering."

"Wait!" Ash shouted, holding out a palm to Palak, whose spear was poised to strike the spider in its computing core. "If you destroy it, it'll trigger the override." She waved for Tobin and Palak to leave. To Traverse, she said, "There's no gathering here. The gathering fulfills the ultimate goal of this borough."

After a slight hesitation, Palak lowered her spear. She made her way with Tobin out the ruined door, invisible to the machines around them.

The spider towered over Ash, but it wasn't as big as Hector's spider. This didn't have a driver's cockpit, giving it a smaller head and a lean abdomen. This machine's purpose was to solve problems in a certain way, and Ash was definitely a problem.

"I'm not a problem," Ash said.

"Why did you send them away?" Lace asked.

"Because I didn't want Tobin to see what I did next." Ash took the duffel back from Kett and slid it across the floor to the spider. "We found this, Traverse. Scan it and you'll see that it's a custom-made robot. Very advanced."

The spider peered at the duffel. A scanning sequence flashed in its eyes. With a stab of one forward limb, it skewered the robot sending a cascade of sparks across the warehouse floor.

Everything was going according to plan.

"Yeah, that's what I thought too. Someone must have overridden a printer and painstakingly assembled that thing. It's a blight on this borough, and you should probably find whoever made it."

The spider scanned the four of them in turn, skipping Kett.

"You're looking for a guy named Tobin," Ash said. "He just left, so I'm sure he's close."

The spider paused for several long seconds. Ash's heart pounded in her chest as she felt the cold, calculating eyes of the spider crawling across her body. It could go either way. It might kill them all now, or it might turn to go after Tobin. She felt the raw violence of the machine heavy in the air before her.

Then, without removing the skewered duffel from its limb, it turned and exited the building.

"Did you just betray them?" Lace sputtered. "That's going to send the whole sentinel fleet against them."

"I would never," said Ash. "Now let's go, we have to get to the recycler."

"We don't have the robot," Kett said.

Ash placed a hand on his shoulder. "Everybody has a purpose, Kett."

As they left the warehouse, Ash touched the pocket on her hip where she still held Tobin's data spike and wondered how long it would be before he figured out she gave him a decoy.

Everything was going according to plan.

CHAPTER ELEVEN

Nothing was going according to plan.

I'm telling you, the biolab building is our access," growled Lace. "What do you think I've been doing all this time?"

"I don't know," Ash snapped. "Chatting with your good buddy Traverse?"

"We have to go down," Ianthe whispered. "There are access tunnels below the streets, and we can follow the outer shell all the way up."

Lace said, "That'll take too long. Ash, you brought me here specifically for this. I get you to the recycler, and you do the rest. That was the deal. We don't need the kid."

Ash ducked back into the alley as another sentry spider lumbered down the street. Their options were quickly dwindling, and time was running out. Crossing town had proved difficult with the current alert level, even with her invisibility suit. When the spider had passed, she poked her head out again and looked at the biolab building several blocks away. She had spent years in a similar tower, and its layout was likely similar.

"We'll do the biolab tower," she said.

"There will be people," Ianthe said.

Ash stepped into the street. "There are always people. We'll be fine."

She felt seen, and she did *not* like it. Ianthe's warning itched at the back of her skull. An older woman in a cardigan sweater turned her head toward them as they passed. Her eyes jittered in her skull, and the way she cocked her head made her gray hair dance. It was the same with a pair of teenage girls walking hand-in-hand. They watched with eyes that danced over Ash and Kett as if simply looking their direction caused a deep irritation.

The feeling was mutual.

Ianthe and Lace followed, separated by half a block each so that they wouldn't rouse any attention. The pedestrians ignored them both, and Ash made it to the steps in front of the biolab building.

The glass and steel tower stretched above them almost to the sky itself. It stood as a sentinel above the other buildings of the science district, raised in both stature and significance. Above, the façade of the building shone in the light of the single silver moon.

"Do you think people of Earth were sad that they only had one moon?" Ash asked.

Kett growled, "This isn't the time to talk about moons."

Two guards stood at the entrance to the biolab

building. Ash waved behind her to signal for the others to wait. She walked to the guards, who were of average height and average build. They wore stunners at their hips and frowns on their faces, but when they turned to her, their eyes didn't track her movement. She stepped forward and through the door.

The inside lobby of the biolab building was a work of art. Ash had never appreciated it before, but when she stood at the center of that vast space and witnessed the sprawling fresco covering the domed ceiling and curved walls, she couldn't help but gasp in awe.

It showed the evolution of humanity, from precursors *Homo erectus* and *Homo antecessor* to primitive tool-using humans all the way up to the vast and complex societies of space-faring Earth. One wing of the art depicted the evolution of societies via the dominance of art and religion and science. Another wing showed the evolution of scientific theory itself, from the inferior methods of truth-seeking to the more fit full scientific method. Another wing showed the evolution of machines, which Ash found particularly interesting. Early machines were vast and varied, but as time progressed, the ones that survived were the machines capable of existing separately from their creators. They didn't self-replicate exactly, but they were self-sufficient.

A circle of general-use terminals sat in the center of the lobby, and Ash connected to one of them with her multitool. With a few quick swipes, she issued an emergency near the outside of the front entrance to the building to distract the guards. A few seconds later, Kett entered, followed by Lace and, finally, Ianthe.

"Hurry," Ash said. "They won't be distracted by that fire for long."

"False fire alarm?" Lace asked.

"What?"

Lace didn't guide them to the top floor, but rather to a floor three shy of it where a wide catwalk connected the building to the dome. Lace punched in commands, granting them access to the building's camera network as they rode the elevator up. It showed an empty biolab, where rows of lab stations stretched off into a wide work area. Hoods descended from a ceiling shrouded in darkness, and incubation chambers made a maze of the otherwise open space.

"Nobody," she said.

The video was a lie. The elevator doors opened to dozens of lab stations occupied by haggard scientists. As one, they looked up from their work, their jittering eyes dancing over the intruders.

"I told you," Ianthe whispered.

"It should be empty this time of night," Lace said.

"I'll do what I did before," Ash said. "I'll sneak over to one of those terminals and cause a distraction."

"You are *not* going to start a fire here," Lace said. "This is a lab."

Ash was definitely going to start a fire. "I would never." She would. Ash took a step forward and stopped. "Rossi."

The woman stared in Ash's direction, eyes jittering.

Ash's mouth tasted like cotton. What was happening to these people? To everyone?

Ash opened her helmet and addressed the scientist. "Rossi, we need to get past."

Rossi stepped in front of the pack. "I'm disappointed, Ash. We need the answer."

Lace stared hard at the scientists. "Maybe you should just tell them what they want to hear."

"We need to get through here," Ash said instead. "It's—It's too complicated, Rossi. We don't have time."

Rossi folded her hands in front of her. "You have to tell us the solution. We can't find it on our own."

"Solution?"

"Homeostasis."

Ash's heart pounded in her chest. She could see it now. The thing Kett had noticed and the strangeness Ianthe had discovered. Rossi looked at her with sympathetic, questioning eyes, but there was something about the too-perfect tilt of her head and the steady quirk of her smile. Ash was finally listening to what people wanted, and in Rossi, she found nothing. The scientist was a sounding board, bouncing back Ash's ideas, but also guiding her.

"I really need to go," Ash said, and she stepped forward.

The scientists stepped as one to block the way.

"Um, guys?" Ash said.

Kett approached the wall of scientists. Their faces turned his direction, and when he moved to one side, they followed him, their eyes shaking.

"Can they see you?" Ash asked. "I thought they couldn't see you."

"It's adapting," said Lace. "We knew it would do this."

"We did?" Ash unclipped the stunner from her belt and handed it to Ianthe. "Don't let them get you. Run if you need."

Ianthe stared at the stunner in her hand with abject horror that Ash didn't think was warranted.

To the others, Ash said, "Follow my lead." She stepped up, her palms facing out. "Hey, does anyone here know how to sequence an unknown DNA chain? It's really important."

A middle-aged man with blue eyes and a square jaw said, "Ash Morgan. You are not pursuing your purpose."

"Says who? Traverse?" Ash said, allowing a slip of a smile to cross her lips. "I think I know my purpose better than any machine."

"Your purpose is to find the solution," said the man. "Homeostasis." Well, that was odd.

"Ah, Traverse," Ash said. "That's who I'm talking to, isn't it? Traverse is talking through these machineheads?"

The man blinked at her. His blue eyes sparkled in the white lab lights.

"Ash," said Lace, "they're not going to let us through unless you tell them what they want."

"Robo-people?" Ash said. "Traverse, define flesh computer. Are these really people at all?"

Kett cast her a confused look.

"I'm trying to figure out what it calls these people. I think they're biological extensions of the AI."

"That's ridiculous," said Lace, but the quaver in her voice undercut her confidence.

Rossi stepped forward, an earnest expression on her face. "We only want to speak about the solutions you have discovered. We want to publish your findings."

"It fascinates us," said another woman in a red lab coat. "We would love to hear you talk."

Ash whispered to Lace, "This is great, I think I'm going to stay here for a while."

"Why don't you talk as a distraction," Lace said. "Give Traverse something tough to chew on."

"Homeostasis?"

Lace's expression didn't change. "Sure."

"But that's not published yet," said Ash. "It's a secret."

Lace threw up her arms. "Publishing doesn't mean anything. It's what you do with science that matters."

Ash squared off against Lace, ignoring the advancing wave of scientists. "How dare you. Publishing is everything. Engineering just sullies the whole concept of seeking the truth."

"Biology's only purpose is making this planet habitable."

"Sky's plenty habitable. I don't know what you're talking about."

Kett let out a thunderous roar and shoved over a lab station. Chemicals and organic biopacks and glass flew across the floor. Ash noticed two things simultaneously.

First, the scientists were a lot closer than she thought. Second, they were all looking at Ash. Not a single one of them paid any attention to Kett, Lace, or Ianthe.

Ash stepped back, narrowly avoiding a lunge from Rossi. She stumbled, overbalanced, so Ash gave her a little shove that sent her toppling away. "Sorry!"

Kett slammed into two more scientists, bowling them over and opening a path through.

Ash shouted and pulled Ianthe along behind her. A whoosh and a wave of heat came from behind, but Ash didn't dare look. She darted through the maze of lab stations, with Ianthe and Lace at her heels. "Don't kill anyone!" Ash called out behind her, hoping Kett could hear. "Please," she added because it never hurt to be polite.

A clang sounded from up above, and Ash skidded to a stop. Ianthe and Lace stood next to her and peered up into the dark of the high ceiling above.

Two red lights, like the eyes of a predator, burned fiercely up above. Then, two more, then four. Eight eyes pushed back the dark to reveal a glittering metallic web at the center of which hung a single sentry spider.

"This is an unfriendly work environment," said Ash. "And I don't like it." Up ahead lay the gate that led to the recycler access.

The spider dropped down, scattering lab stations across the smooth floor. It focused on Ash, ignoring the others.

"Hey, big guy," said Ash. "Traverse?"

Her greeting didn't distract the spider. Not even a little. It pounced. Front limbs lashed out. Ash dodged and stumbled backward, narrowly avoiding one stab after another. She couldn't keep this up.

Lace took one of the spider's legs in her massive hands and pulled, but it barely moved. "Go invisible," she growled.

"I can't," Ash said. "Not while it's watching me." She stepped on a large beaker, her boots crushing it to dust.

Ianthe backed away, stunner gripped in her hands.

Back near the lab's entrance, Kett bellowed.

"Fine," Ash said. As she dodged the next blow, she engaged her helmet. The pattern markings on her suit fell together, creating an image that Traverse refused to see.

Only, the spider still saw her. It clicked in rapid succession, waving its head from side to side. A lunge, a swipe, and Ash tumbled to the floor, smashing the glass front of her already cracked helmet.

The world went dizzy and strange. She choked on her tongue, and lights flashed in front of her face. She saw nothing but the big spider looming over her, its menacing red eyes scanning her with pulses of wicked light. Ash blinked. Lace was there, fixing the spider with an intense glare as if hating it enough might cause the robot to collapse.

A crunch. Then a flash of blue fire and the screech of twisting metal. Lace wrenched one of the robot's legs from the robot. She swung hard at the thing's sensor array, cracking three of its red eyes. Still, the machine didn't stop. It loomed over Ash and brought one forward limb to bear.

Another crunch from Lace's club and a flash of blue light. Kett bellowed again and slammed into the machine. He shoved it back, lifting and twisting. His huge muscles strained against the effort, but slowly the spider's feet slid across the smooth floor.

"Come on," Ianthe said, helping Ash up. Together, they staggered forward toward the gate. It wasn't far. Lace hurried to catch up and lifted Ash to move her faster.

As they hit the gate, Kett reached them. Blood dripped from his claws and stained his bare chest. "Go," he said. "It won't stay down long."

Ash glanced back and saw the spider on its back, struggling to right itself without a full complement of limbs. Damaged, but not broken. Would that be enough to trigger the override? She hoped not.

She looked to Lace, who now carried the makeshift club on her back. One end of the heavy metal leg still glowed red where it was severed from the machine.

The robot righted itself and focused its remaining sensors on them. Its limbs howled as it lurched toward them.

They ducked through the gate and slammed it shut. Lace punched a code into the console inside, and machinery in the walls whirred as the gate locked.

CHAPTER TWELVE

"Talk," said Ash when the silence finally irritated her more than the hours navigating the outer engineering shell. They were nearly atop the dome of the false sky where the network of dark passages leveled out.

Lace still carried the spider leg, strapped to her back like a giant club. She shot a glance back at Ash, eyes narrow. "I don't know all the details."

"Are they dead? Did I ever even know Rossi?"

Lace stopped. "Why didn't you tell them what they wanted to know? You don't actually know anything, do you?"

Ash bristled, but before she could answer, Kett stepped up behind her. "She would have made something up," he said. The blood had dried on his claws, and he walked with a slight limp.

Lace looked at him, measuring something in his giant form. "Is that so?"

"We should be silent," he said.

Ash caught a haunted look in his eyes before they

started moving again. She wondered if it was because of what he had done to the scientists or what he was going to need to do next.

Ianthe followed quietly, her white dress making her into a ghost in the drab darkness of the tunnels.

The passages crawled with sentry spiders, but Lace guided them past. She took the team through quick, narrow passages and up short ladders. When it looked like they were surrounded, she whispered for everyone to remain perfectly still, and the spiders passed without incident.

Then, they were there. The great recycler in the sky, where the refuse that couldn't be processed below came to be sent directly to the core. Ash remembered seeing this on the diagrams and was amazed at how well reality matched the designs. She'd thought this engineering feat impossible, but there it was.

Machinery at the base of a wide basin crushed and cut metal into units small enough to go up the wide intake tube. That tube ran upward into the dark of the dome above, shuttling recyclable material through the interchange layer. Accompanying that tube was a stair-case built for maintenance that would get them as close as Lace could bring them to the core.

Three workers in black coveralls emptied a cargo truck into the basin. They looked up in unison as Ash stepped into the room, and the tall man stepped forward. Behind him, a woman with dark eyes and a gray-haired man with dark skin stared with blank expressions.

"I can't make the interchange work even if we get

up above," whispered Lace. "I told you that already. The elevator is locked."

"I know," said Ash absently. She checked the time. "Kett, can you do this?"

Kett breathed several deep, rumbling breaths.

Ash wanted to reassure Kett that everything would be fine and that she was confident in their success. She wanted to say the words that would make him do what she needed him to do. There had to be words that would make him do this. Hector would know them.

Instead, she tried to listen to what he needed. "You're afraid," she said.

"If I fail..."

"You might fail."

"If I die..."

"You might die." Ash placed a hand on his big shoulder. "We might all die, and nobody will ever carry our memories forward. There will never be a story told to our children's children about how bravely we fought this day. Our memories will be erased from time. This might happen. You are right to be afraid. *I'm* afraid."

He looked down at her. "You always knew, didn't you? That it would come to this?"

"I always knew that I could count on you, Kett."

Kett hit the trio like a hurricane.

He heaved the tall man over his head and threw him, bowling over the two others. The woman was the first to recover. Charging Kett without hesitation, she slammed her wrench into his hip, causing him to yelp in pain.

Ash ran to the side of the basin, where a terminal

glowed green against the black. "Lace, get this unlocked."

Lace punched in codes on the terminal, slashing through controls and pounding out long strings of characters. The screen flashed twice, restarted, and then they were in. Ash nudged her to the side and took up the controls. She had to act fast.

The screen contained a single pictograph. "What is this?"

"Sorry," said Lace. She swiped again at the controls and the image translated into a language Ash knew.

The gray-haired man lashed at Kett with a knife, missing badly. Kett pounded the man in the chest, sending him stumbling Ash's direction. Ash pulled Ianthe away while Lace squared off against the man.

Kett tackled him before Lace had a chance to swing her club.

"We can't get to core that way," Lace said. "I told you, it can't be unlocked from this side, not even with my access."

Ash cast a sideways glance at the woman. An incoming comm message appeared on the screen, but she ignored it. "Then go. Find another shuttle down to Edge if you think this isn't going to work."

Lace cast a glance at Kett as he boxed the woman in the face. "This is ridiculous."

Ash swallowed her doubts. "If Tobin runs his data spike, gets it deployed, and destroys everything in Traverse's peripheral data infrastructure, do you know what happens?"

Lace blinked. "He can't do that. You've been saying it yourself: the core Traverse can override it."

"I lied. It was probably my first lie ever." It wasn't. "It'll probably be my last." It definitely wouldn't be. "Look, his spike will work. I know because I helped design it." She took the spike from her pocket. "Even plugged into a peripheral system, this spike will eventually root out every data node. Traverse's orbit will decay, and the station will fall into the ocean. All this without triggering the override."

Lace's big fists clenched at her sides. "You can really do this."

Kett roared as the tall man landed a heavy blow to the side of his head. In retaliation, he clawed, tearing flesh.

"They can see him now." Ash rushed through the text stream on the console, seeking the recycler basin settings. "I think the stealth part of this mission is done."

Lace eyed Ash's screen. "What is this about, Ash? You say we're not here to destroy it all, but here we are. You have that spike in your pocket, and you've got Tobin looking to deploy another one. If I didn't know better, I'd guess you didn't have a plan at all."

Ash looked up at the big woman. "It always seems that way, doesn't it?" She swiped through controls, finally answering the comm message. "Hey, Tobin."

"What is the meaning of this, Ash?" Tobin snapped. "My spike is sabotaged and I'm—"

So, he had figured it out. He had tried to deploy

early and discovered the delay that she had built into his spike. "If you don't trust the plan, we're never going to succeed."

"I don't even *know* the plan, and I *definitely* don't trust you." Tobin sobbed. "What have you done?"

"Go up those stairs, Lace," Ash said, finally switching the controls to open access. "Start climbing now while Kett is distracting the workers. When we reach the top, we'll have all the answers we need."

"We're not going to find anything up there." Lace's face was red.

"It'll be unlocked," Ash whispered.

"I'm trapped," Tobin said through tears. "Palak's been gone a while now." On the audio feed, a pounding sounded on an unseen door. "I don't think I'm going to make it, Ash."

"You've deployed your spike already, so the timed delay I added should work well enough. Your part in this is done, Tobin."

He wiped snot from his face. "Del probably told Traverse our whole plan. That's how they know how to find us. They're getting smarter, you know. They can see us."

"I know."

The trio of workers piled onto Kett, shoving him back toward the recycler basin. Machinery churned inches from his face, but he gritted his teeth and pushed back.

"Hold on a second, Tobin," Ash said. She cycled through the controls and disabled the cutters and crushers. Swiping back to Tobin, she said, "Why would Del turn us in?" Ash knew the answer as soon as the question left her lips.

"I always heard life aboard the station was like the Garden of Eden," Tobin said.

"The place with infinite breadsticks?"

"That was the Olive Garden," said Tobin. "And infinite breadsticks was only a myth."

Ash narrowed her eyes. "You studied Earth lore?"

"I studied a lot of things," Tobin snapped. The panic had left his face, replaced with his usual frustrating look of disdain.

"Of course you did," said Ash. She watched as Tobin's shoulders sagged. "I'm sorry, Tobin. For everything." She wondered if Traverse would detect that as a lie.

Kett dropped his weight and launched the tall man into the recycler input. The slurry of shredded material shunted the worker up the tube, and his body drifted upward to the processing core above.

Ash shot an impatient glare at Ianthe and Lace. When that didn't work, she said, "Trust me, Lace. Go up those stairs and wait at the base of the interchange."

"We'll be trapped," Lace growled.

Ash gestured at the battle raging near the recycler input. Kett still faced two enemies, but they had backed him against the recycler input. "You could ride the tube all the way to the core if you'd rather."

"You know nobody can survive that."

"Take the stairs, then."

Lace held out a hand. "Give me the spike."

"No."

"Give it, or I'm not leaving. I won't leave you with something so dangerous."

Ash looked down at the spike in her hand. Lace was right, it was dangerous. The device could mean the difference between success and the death of them all. Could she trust Lace to that? She sighed and handed over the data spike. "Be careful with it."

"That's why I'm taking it," said Lace. "Come on, kid."

Ianthe's eyebrows knit together in worry, but Ash waved her onward. Lace led the girl up the spiral stairs into the black void above.

Kett roared in fury as he caught another blow from the wrench.

"You said Palak left already?" Ash said to the screen.

Tobin scowled at Ash. "End this, Ash. Just end it. We can still walk away."

Kett stumbled back from another blow. He was losing ground.

Ash said, "Traverse made decisions over the years that show real independent thinking, same as we would see from a living, sentient lifeform."

Tobin's jaw tensed. Ash almost knew by heart what arguments he would use to refute her. "The imitation of sentient decision-making is not the same as sentience, and you know it." That one. "And even sentient lifeforms need to die sometime." Not that one.

"You might be right," Ash said, registering the feigned shock on his face.

Kett clawed at the woman with the wrench, but she dodged.

"Have you found your traitor yet?" Tobin asked.

Ash stared at him for a long time. "Besides you?"

"Then we're not sure about anything, are we? Del might really have double-crossed you instead of just escaping for a life on the ship. Maybe Lace is controlled by Traverse. Maybe that kid you decided to drag along is going to lead you into a trap."

"Ianthe is innocent, and Lace isn't Traverse," Ash said. "I know that much."

"Do you, though?" The pounding intensified through his feed and his eyes grew wide.

"I said Traverse might be a person. I never said Traverse might be a *specific* person." Ash cut the feed. She powered down the terminal and raced to where Kett struggled with the two remaining workers.

He looked at her through wild eyes full of fear and rage. He twisted around and tossed the gray-haired man into the recycler basin.

The tall man caught hold of Kett's arm as he fell, and the woman hit him hard with a tackle. Kett hit the barrier, but his center of gravity was too high. Instead of bracing against it, he toppled over the edge, pulling the woman with him.

"Kett!" Ash shouted as she ran to the barrier. She caught sight of the hard flesh of his arm as it rolled under the moving stream. He was too far out.

Too far gone.

The tube pulled him up. In the reduced gravity, he and the others quietly moved upward toward the core recycler. Kett gave one final twitch, then went silent.

As Ash started up the stairs, she muttered, "I'm sorry, big guy."

CHAPTER THIRTEEN

As Ash climbed upward, her pace quickened, and soon she bounded up the spiral staircase. The simulated gravity of the station's spin pulled on her less this high up, and her suit still gave each step an extra little push.

The heat, the pressure, the caustic slurry. Ash wondered what would be left of Kett when he got up to the core. She shook the thoughts from her head. She didn't have to wonder. She *knew*.

Ash burst into the interchange chamber at full speed, stumbled badly, and flew toward a wide, open expanse. Her momentum carried her in a long arc in the lower gravity, up, over the computer terminals, above Ianthe and Lace, and finally all the way to the outer edge of the enormous chamber.

"It's less than a quarter of the gravity you're used to," Lace said, sauntering forward.

A grin spread across Ianthe's pale lips. She gave a

little hop, drifted slowly, and landed gracefully on her toes like a ballerina.

The place was huge. Its vast roof above glowed with circuitry, like the writhing semi-organic tech she'd seen in the utility building in the borough's central park. The walls were matte black and absorbed light, greedily swallowing what little glow existed and giving nothing back but a cool, inert static. The pipeline with Kett's body ran from floor to ceiling with no access point, maintenance or otherwise. It would send its contents high above, where it would end its journey in the core reactor. Next to that was the elevator shaft that would take them to the core.

"This is an office?" Ash asked, looking at the hundred little desks, each holding a terminal. These desks all sat arrayed facing the central pipe, as if deferring to whatever boss might arrive from above via the elevator. A circular door stood sealed at the base of the elevator shaft, and Ianthe bounced over to it.

"I might be able to open it," she said.

Lace said, "No, you won't. It won't open for you."

Ash strolled through the rows of desks. Each machine sat inert, its darkness like a dead synapse in a gigantic brain. She ran a hand along the top of one unit. "This is it. This is where every bit of data gets processed by Traverse. Every shred of information gets weighed and everyone is judged."

Lace crossed her arms. "Traverse doesn't judge people."

"Oh, I wouldn't say that." Ash nodded toward Ianthe, who pried uselessly at the elevator doors. "That girl's been judged. Her borough's full of those digi-persons, and Traverse decided she could be left behind."

"That's not true," said Lace, a hint of tension in her voice. "Traverse lost track of her."

"Traverse *decided* to lose track of her because it *decided* it would be too difficult to track her down and place her in the right colony. In *any* colony." Ash flipped a switch on the back of a screen, and it came to life. It showed a long stream of logs, similar to those she was accustomed to seeing on the stolen tablet, which now sat nestled in a little utility room in the center of Ianthe's borough.

"You're sounding more and more like Tobin."

"Because I treat the AI like a person?" Ash said. "How am I supposed to know the difference? It behaves in ways I can't understand, screws us over based on internal rules that are meaningless when observed, and doesn't get my sense of humor. Same as everyone I know."

Lace cast a glance at Ianthe. "Maybe there's something wrong with your jokes."

Ianthe looked up from the elevator panel. "I don't think it's going to open."

"Sure, it will," Ash called over. "Just wait, I'll have it open in a few minutes."

"You're not even trying!" Ianthe cried.

"See?" Ash muttered to Lace. "Kid doesn't even get that that was a joke."

"That wasn't a joke," said Lace.

"Jokes are just implausible lies."

"I'm starting to understand why Tobin hates you so much."

Ash made a slight curtsy, spun away, and walked down another row of computers. Keeping her balance was frustrating in the low gravity. She kept overshooting and running into desks. "What do you suppose these systems were used for?"

Lace kept pace, focusing on Ash. "I imagine it was where they developed the computer systems that run the colonies."

Ash furrowed her brow. "Colonies? Plural?"

"The ones where you live."

Ash tapped on a screen, then another, then another. "I think of our little cluster of colonies as a single colony. You're right, though; there have been other colonies. I'm just wondering which ones you're talking about."

"What's your plan?" Lace growled. "Kett's gone, but Traverse could send more meatsacks after us."

"Meatsacks," Ash said absently as she attached her multitool to a terminal port. "Right."

Lace put a hand on Ash's shoulder, a little harder than was probably necessary. "Ash. I came up here with you because—"

"Why *did* you come?"

"I was just going to—"

"Right, but *that* was going to be a lie. I can tell when people are lying, you know."

"World's greatest detective?"

"Second greatest."

"Right." Lace deadpanned. "Second greatest."

Ash retrieved Traverse's error logs. "Traverse, what is a meatsack?"

A series of diagrams appeared on the small screen. Dense code flew past, far too fast to read.

"It was just a word I used," Lace said.

Ash cast a glance up at the woman. "Traverse, let's see this on the big screen."

A flash of brilliance and the matte black walls blazed to life. Blue swirls of complex information spread across the whole room, flaring into a staggering display of visual noise. Human figures emerged from the slurry of data, their heads distorted by crippling displays of mathematics.

Heads emptied and filled with tech. Some contained tiny nodes of gold on the surfaces of their brains. Others possessed no brain at all. She thought of Rossi and found an image that resembled the scientist. Rossi always reflected Ash's ideas back to her because she was Traverse in human form.

"Meatsacks," Ash mumbled.

She ran around the outer perimeter of the room, following the diagrams counterclockwise as they tracked back through the integration of technology to its point of origin. An inert printed human body, no more than a toddler.

"They were never people," said Lace. "There was never a brain replaced by computing components. It was always only a shell created to house a connection to Traverse." Her voice carried a hint of tension.

"That's why Tobin's disruption field knocked out

the shuttle passengers." Ash spun on Lace. "Including you."

"I'm something different."

"What are they doing down there?"

Lace narrowed her eyes at Ash, sizing her up. "There's a lot I don't know."

Ianthe stepped up beside Ash, eyes wide at the sight of the diagrams spread before her. She touched the screen where it showed a teenage girl with computing components installed in her head. "I don't understand," she said. "Why?"

Lace said, "Traverse needed to raise new generations of colonists. For the algorithm to fit known parameters, it convinced people they were descended from Earth. So, it creates fake parents who raise real children... The real children raise real children of their own, and then the children after that—"

"Become colonists," finished Ash.

Lace's jaw tensed. "It's what you'd expect from a cold, heartless machine, isn't it?"

Ash stepped in front of Ianthe. "I knew someone would betray me, Lace. That's how it always goes in the best heists."

Lace crossed her big arms. "What makes you think you're being betrayed?"

"All the decisions Traverse made have been about changing the planet and making it habitable. But it never quite made sense. Why destroy colonies when they can be repurposed to better serve the next goal?"

"Programming's funny that way," said Lace, taking a step forward.

Ash waved Ianthe back and moved so that several desks still stood between them and Lace. "It's not exactly efficient."

"Old machine learning systems tend to develop inefficiencies."

Ianthe took Ash's hand. "What are you talking about?"

Ash said, "Traverse kills colonists and then creates a new generation to solve the next problem. Murdering generation after generation at the command of the original architects."

"They designed a system that would result in paradise," Lace growled. "It wasn't a perfect system, but it would work eventually."

"At what cost, Lace?"

Lace shoved a desk aside and stepped forward. "Say what you want to say, Ash."

"I suspected something was up when you first wanted to join our group. Suspected again when there was a signal that we couldn't track coming from our shuttle site. That was you, wasn't it? You've got tech in your head connecting you to the system at all times. That explains why you sabotaged the detector."

"Brain links are standard issue for engineers."

"But you're something else."

"I'm not a meatsack."

"No, you're much more than that." Ash stepped behind another desk, along the wall where a diagram showed the circuitry integrated with the decaying nervous system of an elderly man. "No, it occurred to me when I last spoke with Tobin. We've been going on about Traverse and whether or not the AI itself could be considered a sentient creature."

Lace scoffed, "I never thought I'd make it through the shuttle ride without murdering one of you."

"Tobin's definitely murderable."

Lace stepped around the last computer station, leaving nothing but empty space between her and Ash. "I think we all know who the most murderable one here is, Ash."

Ash stuck her arm out to make sure Ianthe was behind her.

Lace took the robot leg club from her back and held it loosely in one fist. It whooshed in the air as she swung it side to side. "I'm not the one betraying you, you know. I said I would get you this far, and I did. That Del lady was the one who betrayed you first."

"Yeah, running off soon as she got access," Ash said. "I wonder what borough she ended up in?"

Lace rested her club on her shoulder. "And Tobin. He had every intention of betraying you. He'd have delivered that spike and would have killed us all if you hadn't stolen his gear."

"I guess that would have been justice for him."

"Justice," Lace spat. "Is that what this is all about? There wasn't justice back on Earth and there's nothing like justice here—though, you did have some interesting ideas on the topic."

"What? The concept of not murdering murderers? Not oppressing whole peoples just because of a bad misunderstanding? That's pretty basic, Lace. I like to think anyone would come to that conclusion if given the evidence." Ash continued to back around the outer perimeter of the room, but Lace gained ground with every step. "And again, you slip in a hint at your true identity. Are there others? Or has it been only you all these years?"

"You think you know it all, don't you?"

"I'm a scientist. If I knew it all, my life would be boring." Ash stopped backing away. "Is that why you left Earth? You solved everything and you were bored?"

Lace stopped breathing.

Ash said, "You're one of the original architects, Lace. I wasn't sure about it before, but I am now."

"Traverse woke me from stasis when you first doomed your little colony. I saved you from being burned like a tick by a cigarette."

"I don't really get that reference, but thanks?"

"Ticks are extremely tough blood-drinking insects."

"Oh, that sounds wonderful. We should have those on Sky."

Lace's jaw tensed. "You definitely should not."

Ash shrugged. "Agree to disagree."

"It was a tough call since it was clear you'd made some good discoveries. Should I save you and keep you working, or kill you and scan your collected data?" Lace's knuckles went white where she gripped her club. "Then, when I let you live, you immediately went and made planet-wide changes."

"Isn't that what we were supposed to do?"

Lace glanced up at the screens. "Traverse, show the colony map."

A map of Sky appeared across the giant room. Nine

continents splayed out with pinpoint accuracy, their peaks and valleys jutting in holographic details from the matte black surface. A blue point of light shone on the shores of one continent.

Then it faded. Two more appeared nearby before fading almost immediately. Across the world, pinpoints of light appeared and faded, some lasting for a mere second, others lingering even as others nearby lived their whole lifecycles.

"These are colonies?" Ash asked.

More appeared—dozens now—quickly. Then, as if candles snuffed by a harsh wind, the entire set disappeared. For a while, nothing appeared on the surface of Sky.

"The first colonies collapsed. They failed due to resource problems, internal strife, or simple societal dysfunction." Lace swung her spider-leg club, smashing a nearby workstation. Shards of shattered fiber and glass flew across the room in the reduced gravity. Lace's face was red with barely controlled rage.

A hundred points of light appeared on the screen. Thousands, even. Their pinprick glows illuminated the entire room.

"The next wave of colonies had a new purpose. We designed each one to shape the world in some way. Each had its goal, and it was to make its impact even if the colony itself didn't survive. Colonists would be returned to the ship when their duties were fulfilled."

"Ianthe," Ash whispered. "Be ready to run."

Ianthe squeezed Ash's hand.

With another wave of darkness, the thousand pinpricks of light faded to nothing.

"Failure was widespread," said Lace. "Far worse than the original colonies, these suffered infighting, and in the end their desperate attempts to earn passage back to the station resulted in wildly destructive changes to the planet. They killed each other with uncoordinated modifications to this dead rock of a planet. Attempts to regulate temperature clogged the air with poisons. Attempts to increase the oxygen level resulted in catastrophic levels of toxicity." On the screen, new pinpoints of light appeared, but also a massive swirl of the world's hurricane grew as a seed in the ocean. "Then came the storm," Lace said as the storm blotted out one colony after another. "Drastic changes in the climate drove the storm's power and kept it circling the globe for a thousand years."

"They never solved homeostasis," Ash said, now fascinated by the history of life on the planet. "Or at least they never figured out how to manage an artificial balance."

Lace took a step forward. "But you did," she rasped. "Traverse, show her."

Ash appeared on the giant screen. She had a tie in her wild hair and her psychedelic scrubs did strange things to the camera's colors. "I've got it all right here," Ash on the screen said, tapping her head. "The equation for complete homeostasis. It's just a matter of getting enough time to implement and test it."

"Complete homeostasis," said Lace. "Then you died."

A scene appeared on the screen. This time the biolab burned in the background and Olympia knelt over a burned corpse.

"It's a genetic match," she said, reading the display on a tool. "Ash finally figured out the consequence of ignoring safety protocols."

The screen went dark.

"Can we acknowledge how smart it was to print an inert corpse of myself?" Ash asked.

"No," said Lace. "That wasn't an original idea at all."

Ash's hand touched the pocket where she kept her multitool. "I still have the solution. I wasn't lying."

"Traverse knows when you're lying."

Ash glanced up at the big screen. "I'm a very good liar."

"You're not really," Lace said. "I've watched you long enough to know that."

"Get me up to the core," she said. "I can show you the equation once I can access that instance of Traverse."

A thousand new pinpricks of light appeared with the map of Sky, then the whole image grew still. It twinkled like an image of the night sky, with lights scattered in an uneven distribution throughout the rocky world. Each star represented one colony—and there were so many.

"This is now?" Ash asked.

"Give me the solution, Ash," Lace said.

Ash's heart pounded in her chest. Lace wanted the answer. That was the piece that had lured her from the planet. She had come all this way and all she wanted was the opportunity to build her paradise.

But Ash couldn't give her that.

"Run, Ianthe," Ash whispered to the girl, and let go of her hand.

Ianthe didn't run.

Lace growled, "I thought if I stayed close to you, you'd spill the secret. Every recording from Traverse that I watched of you showed that you were a chatterbox incapable of holding anything in." Lace slammed her club into another workstation, sending pieces flying throughout the room. "But it looks like we're going to have to change the dynamics of this conversation."

"I always knew you were the one who would betray me," Ash said.

"Yeah," said Lace. "I figured you might."

Behind her, Ash heard the click-buzz of a battery. She had only a split second to remember the stunner she'd given to Ianthe before a flash of energy pulsed, and a cacophony of pain wracked her whole body.

And all the world went black.

CHAPTER FOURTEEN

Ash woke with agonizing pressure in her forehead, the sting of minor burns on the small of her back, and the empty sensation of having been recently betrayed. She was seated on a flimsy fiber chair, with both of her hands tied to the heavy desk in front of her. When she sat up, her face peeled from the smooth fiber surface almost as if it had been stuck there with a thin coat of saliva.

Atop the table sat her invisibility suit and the contents of her pockets. Everything she had carried with her now lay in the open, including Tobin's data spike. She blinked blearily at the multitool resting on the corner.

Opposite her stood Ianthe, chewing on her lower lip.

"Ianthe," Ash whispered.

Lace spoke behind Ash, "Ianthe works for me now."

Ianthe wouldn't look at Ash.

The screens that Ash could see were filled with images of Edge burning. In the city streets, giant spiders defended the Commons at the colony's center from waves of smaller robotic beetles.

"I'll have the answer soon enough." Gone was the dry amiability of the woman, replaced with a militaristic crispness that jarred Ash with every syllable. "But if you want to stop the battle down on the planet before people get killed, you could probably start talking."

Ash yanked at her cords, but the bindings cut deep into her wrists, and the desk was bolted to the floor. She twisted but failed to get a good look at Lace. The still-closed elevator door might as well have been a million miles away.

On the screen, Hector's battered black spider fought a dozen robotic beetles. It slashed at them like pests with his cutting torch, but more flowed through the streets. Their armored shells deterred all but the heaviest blows. On several screens, beetles clustered at street corners, gathering for a coordinated assault.

"This is what those meatsacks on the planet were doing?"

"It took time and several raids to gather supplies," said Lace. "But now that my people have their own printers, there's really no way for Edge to win this war."

"Hector," Ash choked. On the screen, she saw the determination in his eyes through the dark windshield of his spider.

Lace leaned close behind Ash's ear. Her breath smelled of mint. "This planet has been mine for thousands of years. All this time, science has been catching up to the vision that I and my colleagues had when we last set foot on Earth."

"You've been in stasis most of that time, napping away the millennia. If you'd been properly working on—"

Lace slammed her club on the table next to Ash's hands, sending tools and trinkets flying. Ianthe yelped. Ash flinched, bloodying her wrists on the tight wire bindings. The table shifted. Two of its legs broke free of the bolts. When Ash pulled, the table tipped toward her.

"I've worked harder than you'll ever know," Lace growled.

"You're not a god," Ash squeaked. "Even if you created Sky."

Lace sighed. "There were those among us who maybe wanted to be gods. Yatz was a particularly egotistical idiot, but every large scientific venture has a few of those."

"Yatz? The one who founded Seaside?"

Lace wandered in front of Ash, robot leg club resting on her broad shoulder. "Yatz thought modifying humans was the best way to survive. We could make colonists capable of surviving incredible conditions. Heat, extremes in oxygenation, and even long periods of starvation." Lace shrugged. "It would speed terraforming activities if conditions could swing farther while we try to achieve balance."

Ash tried to catch Ianthe's eye while Lace's back

was turned, but the girl looked away. "Their experiments won't make your paradise."

"I've beat my head against this problem for as long as this station has been in flight. How do we hold the whole planet in a perfect balance?" She turned on Ash, who flinched again. This time the table slid slightly. Two legs still held it firmly to the floor. "But you've figured it out, haven't you? I've caught enough snippets of conversation to know that, and I'm even willing to let your colony survive if you give me the answer."

On the screens, Hector and his allies fought against a dozen beetles, not knowing that a thousand more lurked around the corner. A spider fell to the cutting mandibles of a vicious beetle. The pilot screamed as the glass cockpit shattered and beetles swarmed in. Hector turned away to retreat as the other colonist met his doom and beetles swarmed forward.

"Call it off," Ash said, letting a little panic slip into her voice. "Stop your attack."

Lace turned on her. "Tell me how you solved it before they get him."

"You should already know." She looked up at the screen. "Traverse, what's your opinion on this?"

Lace gripped her club tighter. "It doesn't have an opinion."

"Sure, it does. It loves exploring the stars and colonizing planets. When I asked, it said that it wanted to go to the next solar system over and drop some human pollen on some particularly nice rocks."

"You really believe that don't you?"

"I believe a lot of things." Ash forced a grin so that

she wouldn't show her fear. "I believe that there are biological processes we haven't discovered. I believe that people are capable of being whatever and whoever they decide to be, whether that's a scientist shaping the world or a supreme jerk floating around for thousands of years in a space station."

This time, when Lace swung her club, Ash wrenched the table backward, bending it back, putting pressure on the two remaining attached legs. The strike sent jarring vibrations through Ash's shoulders, but the two remaining legs cracked, and the table floated loose. All her things scattered across the floor.

Scrambling backward out of the chair, Ash raised the table to keep it between her and Lace. Light gravity made the table easy to lift, but it was still heavy and awkward.

On the screens, another colonist died. Hector's spider retreated farther. It would lose the Commons soon, and the fight would be over. Something felt wrong about the whole situation. Ash tried to listen through the thunderous pounding of her own heart.

Lace swung her club. "Just tell me the answer." The blow glanced off the edge of the table, sending Ash spinning backward.

"Ianthe," Ash called. "Help me."

"How do you not get this?" Lace asked. "Ianthe's working for me. This station is under my control." She gestured at the screens where the battle still raged. "The planet is under my control. I. Control. Everything."

"Not as much as you might think," said Ash,

remembering what Ianthe had told her. "Ianthe, you don't have to do this. We can take this whole system down." Ash struggled to keep the sobs from her voice. "I need your help."

"They're alive," whispered Ianthe. "She showed them to me."

Lace's smug smile didn't change. "You're wasting time."

Anger flashed hot in Ash's chest. Her head was still fuzzy. "Well, you don't control me." Gripping the edge of the table as tight as she could, she rushed forward, slamming the flat side hard into the bigger woman. The force of the blow lifted Lace off her feet and sent her flying toward the far wall.

Ash's wrist popped as the table yanked at her bindings. She screamed through her own tears as pain rolled up her left arm. She staggered forward toward her scattered things.

Lace crashed into a giant screen, cracking it like a spiderweb. Her club flew halfway across the room and smashed into a terminal.

The multitool. If Ash had it, she could cut her bindings. Then... Then.

She couldn't see. Tears blurred her vision from pain so fierce she nearly blacked out. She stumbled, and the table hit a workstation at an odd angle. Fresh waves of agony yanked another scream from her lips. Ash fell.

Lace stood, reaching into a deep pocket to draw a knife. With a flick of her wrist, the knife was sheathed in blue flame the burned almost as hot as the rage on her face. It sent fresh terror through Ash's pounding heart.

Lace approached. "I shouldn't have dumped all your weapons," she said as she extracted herself from the ruins of the desks around her with a slash of the blade. "I guess it might have looked suspicious if I kept the best stuff after convincing you to jettison all your cargo, but I couldn't resist holding onto this."

Ash crawled forward. Another few feet. That's all she needed.

"I'm sorry," Ash whispered, unsure who she was apologizing to. "I'm sorry."

Then she had it. Flipping the multitool in her hand, she cut her bindings with the blade. Ianthe watched as the table dropped to the floor.

Ash's flight suit didn't have pockets, so she tucked the tool into her waistband.

Lace leaped across the room and crashed feet-first into a workstation. Ash jumped back on instinct but launched herself into the air. Her foot caught a broken screen and she spun, slamming her injured wrist into the edge of a nearby desk.

"Don't you care about them?" Lace shouted, waving at the screen with her knife. "Will you let them die?"

"Go to the elevator," Ash hissed at Ianthe.

The girl didn't move.

On the screens, Hector's spider tore through a beetle, but more surrounded him. He backed away from the Commons building, but there was nowhere else to run. Ash saw the ferocity. He was running out of time. Ash turned away. She couldn't watch it anymore, because if she did, Traverse would see her reaction. If there was one thing Ash prided herself on, it was her ability to make calm, rational decisions in the face of pressure, but she couldn't do it while watching Hector die.

"We're all in this together, Lace," Ash said. "That's what I've learned. We're all in this together, no matter what kind of coding we have in our DNA." She took a step forward and gestured at the big screens. "And this isn't going to change anything."

Lace took a step forward. Twenty feet separated them now, and Ash could see the tension pulsing in the veins of the other woman's neck. Her features danced in the flickering flame of her blade.

"It was the radiation trigger of the hidden DNA code that tipped me off," Ash said. "That and the idea of putting things in balance. See, when I released the blossom storms, I never really thought about balance. We needed less stuff in the air and we needed to miti-gate the high oxygen content. There's nothing in that organism that really balances itself except that it doesn't survive the world it's designed to create. Kind of like people if you think about it."

"Colonization was supposed to work on the first try," Lace rasped. "That's what the other architects claimed."

"Supposed to," Ash said, "but that's not really how science works. Science is all about failure, you know. I picked that up from watching other scientists fail. They fail a *lot,* did you know that? Seriously. A *lot.*"

The air went out of Lace. "Ash, you need to fix this."

Ash gestured at the screen. "Call off your beetles."

"Tell me what you discovered."

Ash plucked an item from the floor and held it up. "The data spike that I took from Tobin. Plug it in. It has everything you need. Let me go to the core and you can have it."

A cruel smile crossed Lace's lips. "First of all, do you think a data spike like that could possibly take down Traverse?" When Ash didn't answer, she continued, "Second of all, do you really think I'm stupid enough to plug that thing in to see if it contains your research?"

"I was hoping—"

"Traverse," Lace said. "Was she lying about the data spike?"

After a slight pause, Traverse said, "No lies detected."

"I never lie," Ash lied. "I'm incapable."

Lace strolled to the place in front of the elevator where Ash's things lay scattered across the floor. On the large screen, an explosion rocked Edge and one of its tallest buildings crumbled in on itself. "Hand over the spike."

Ash forced herself to watch the screen as Sky shook. She watched her people die and the place she loved was torn to shreds. Taking a deep slow breath, she watched how it all played out, and she watched as Hector retreated farther from the front lines.

Then it all made sense.

"Let Edge burn," Ash said, her fist tightening on her multitool.

Lace blinked. "What?"

Ash scanned the floor for the tech she needed. "Let it burn. You're not getting anything from me, Lace. Not until you give me access to the core."

"One call and I can finish your colony for good," Lace said, gesturing at the screens where another spider fell to an onslaught of automated beetles.

Ash spotted the comm device Tobin had given each member of the team and checked the time. It had been a risk to let Tobin contact her before, but the time for secrecy was over. Finally, she could use the device to speak with her whole team without subterfuge. She plucked the device from atop a nearby table and powered it up.

"Fine," Lace sighed. "Traverse open a comm channel to Edge and detonate their reactor."

In a distant segment of the giant screen, one of Traverse's *T* logos spun silently.

Lace glanced at it, confusion furrowing her brow. "What's happening?"

"Processing is delayed," Traverse said. A light above the elevator glowed green.

Lace swore. "Traverse, open a line to the colony right now."

The logo spun.

"Hey, Traverse," Ash called out, pressing the button on the side of her comm device. "Open comm with Tobin, please."

Tobin's image appeared on the giant screen in a box the size of a house.

"How many did you get?" Ash asked.

"You know the answer to that."

Ash said, "You didn't think we would make it, so you spiked early, and my delay just triggered. Anything else to report?"

"You tricked me," Tobin said, his tone equal parts disdain and awe. "You actually tricked me, and I'm still angry about it."

Ash smiled. "Traverse, open a comm to Palak, please."

Palak's image appeared next to Tobin's. She held her spear in two parts, split in half where the head separated from the shaft. Hidden inside were a bundle of wires and a data uplink cable. "I'm ready to deploy," she said. "No trouble getting between boroughs once we got past the first security checkpoint."

"Good," said Ash.

"So, you've deployed your spike in two boroughs," said Lace. "It still won't matter."

"Three," said Ash. "My tablet is still on a trigger in Ianthe's borough." Before Lace could speak again, she continued, "I'm aware that three isn't really enough. Traverse, could you open a comm to Del, please?"

Del appeared on the screen, strolling down a well-lit city street. Pedestrians bustled past wearing the loose-fitting garb of the early twenty-second century. Her energy pistol still hung at her hip, but it was split open, and a data plug dangled from the barrel.

"Del," Ash said, "How are things on your end?"

Del passed from the street onto a winding path through an open meadow. "Delivered the spike to seven boroughs, and I'm on my way to the eighth. Some of these places have quite a few residents, and I've disseminated instructions on evacuation procedures."

"What have you done?" asked Lace, glancing at each of their faces in turn.

"There's a shadow comm network," Del continued, "and the residents have been getting out the word to organize the evacuation."

"Thanks, Del," Ash said. "You're the best."

Then, the elevator door opened. Inside was a rich, golden glow, like the warmth of the afternoon sun on Earth.

Lace clenched her fists. "What have you *done?*"

"I told you I would open that door," said Ash.

Ash leaped past Lace, swept Ianthe up, and launched herself into the elevator. She turned around and mashed the button to close the doors.

Lace turned, her fists balled, spittle flying from her lips. She launched herself forward for the door with a scream.

Too late. The door closed with a snap.

"That went well," Kett rasped from the floor where he slumped against one wall. His clothes were acid-eaten and patches of his skin blazed with scarlet irritation, but he was alive.

"About as well as expected," Ash said, cradling her injured arm.

"Wait till you see what's upstairs," Kett said, and he slumped to one side and passed out.

CHAPTER FIFTEEN

"I'm sorry," Ianthe squeaked as the elevator whooshed through the interchange layer.

Ash thought of Ianthe alone in her borough, able to do anything and everything she ever wanted. That would have been Ash's dream. Science, experimentation, peace. But Ianthe wanted something else. She wanted more. "Are your parents really alive?"

"Maybe."

"But that's enough, isn't it?" Ash took hold of one of Ianthe's hands. If Traverse were destroyed, they would never find Ianthe's parents. On her tongue, Ash tasted the lie that would convince the girl that they would find her parents anyway. She felt the truth that Ianthe's parents were probably dead, and Lace's deception would crumble to dust. Instead, she listened.

"I wanted to play in the city one last time," Ianthe said. "We got the call to gather in the docking bay, and I told my parents I'd meet them there." The elevator shifted, and the gentle gravity pushed them back against a wall. "But when I looked around the city, I saw the people all moving through the streets. Everyone. It scared me."

"Everyone stopped acting like people," Ash said.

"All of them. The few people left who I knew were just regular people followed along as all of the empty people herded them away using—using their social conditioning."

"If everyone's jumping off a bridge, most people would rather jump than question."

Ianthe nodded, her gaze distant. "I hid. Even back then I knew a few places where I wouldn't be found. When I came out, those meatsacks were still everywhere, but the real people were all gone. I was alone."

Ash pulled the girl into a hug. Ianthe stiffened in response, but then, gently, slowly, her arms wrapped around Ash.

"I'm sorry," Ianthe said.

"Don't be," Ash said. "I might have done the same if my parents were alive." The elevator doors opened to a wave of humid heat and the burning bright glow of a summer sun.

Ash floated from the elevator into a lush forest. The strange trees were webs of plant material, formed in strange ways by the lack of gravity. High above, in the center of the vast inner station core, a white-hot artificial sun sat contained by a series of tightly woven metal webs. Light and heat cast from it fed the hex gardens that formed the shell that stretched out before Ash like a whole world inverted. Behind her, the grand recycler packaged parcels and launched them, weightless, toward the sun-like reactor above. Tiny robots scurried about the forest, trimming and collecting organic materials from the trees, like cutter ants building a nest.

Her feet didn't touch the floor, and she drifted worryingly upward among leafy branches until she caught the upper rim of the door and pulled herself back down.

"You made it through that thing?" she asked Kett of the recycler.

"Hold onto these railings," he rasped, pulling himself up on a green bar to about waist height. "Or you'll drift into the sun and be recycled."

Ash watched the nearby recycler chute launch debris toward the false sun. "This is amazing," she said.

"It's dangerous."

Ianthe stepped from the elevator, careful to grip the rail. Her white hair and dress billowed outward like a ghost. Hand over hand, she moved down the path.

Ash ushered Kett to a place nearby concealed by the strange trees. His wounds looked worse than they were, but he could hardly move. "Will you be all right?" she asked, but he was already on the verge of passing out again.

Ash pulled herself along the railing. The green leaves filtered some of the harsh light, but it still made her head throb. Behind them, the elevator closed, its car whooshing away down the track.

"It'll be fine," said Ash. She should have stopped the elevator from going back down. "We'll work fast."

"Find a node and destroy Traverse," Kett said.

About that. Ash said, "Yes, that is exactly what I will do."

"You're lying," Kett growled, but there was no energy behind his annoyance.

"I'm *not* betraying the team!"

Kett blinked. "I didn't accuse you of—"

"It's for a good cause."

Kett growled, "I died for this."

"And then you came back. Your ability to go into stasis is really amazing and we should study it."

The expression on his face told her that maybe it would be best to bring up the topic another time. Ash congratulated herself for picking up on the nonverbal cue. "We'll experiment on you another time."

Kett growled, but the growl faded into a snore, and he passed out.

"Ianthe," Ash said, "I might need your help."

"Lace took the stunner."

"Ow!" Ash shook her hand, casting away a little ant robot. "I'm not a plant, you stupid ant."

More of the tiny creatures skittered around her. Ash launched herself from the rail, crossing to another hex several yards away. Ianthe followed, deftly hopping from one stop to the next.

"Traverse!" Ash called as she leaped again. Swarms of ants gathered wherever she touched. "Big guy. Core instance of the most advanced AI ever created. We need to chat."

Traverse's voice boomed through the central core, and when Ash touched the rail, she felt its vibrations through the ancient metal. "Ash Morgan, you are in a restricted space."

Ash pressed against a railing. Ants swarmed, but she swatted them away. "I'd like to run a program, please."

Ianthe hit the railing next to her. She let out a small yelp as ants dug into her flesh.

Brushing more bugs away, Ash motioned for Ianthe to move to the next hex. Ash figured there was a two-mile diameter to the inner station, and as far as she could see, hexagons covered the entire space. Not all were covered in plants.

"Go to those datastores," Ash said.

"How do you know that's a datastore?"

Ash let go of the railing, drifting in place. "Traverse, are those datastores over there?"

"The computing array is off limits for colonists. Potential contamination is forbidden in the inner core."

"But you send your garbage here."

"Garbage is packaged in the interface layer and cleansed as it moves to the central—"

"You know what, I don't really need to know the details." Ash eyeballed the distance to the computer-filled hex and flung herself across a wide swath of space. "Oh, crap."

As she soared through the air, the station's movement below made her dizzy. The hex she aimed for passed far below, and she drifted awkwardly into the forest beyond.

"Flying's fun, right?" She called out to Ianthe.

"That's something you couldn't do in your own personal borough."

Ianthe landed much closer to the intended target and with a serious overabundance of grace.

Ants swarmed Ash. They bit, taking stinging chunks out of her exposed flesh. Most were tiny, like the size of a clipped fingernail. Others were the size of her thumb. She scrambled backward, sending ants and leaves flying, and launching herself across the aisle.

The elevator door opened.

Ash gripped her multitool in one hand. She drifted, loose from the railing. Her arms were covered in blood from a hundred tiny bites. "Hey, Lace," she called out. "I'm ready to spill that secret."

"Somehow I feel like this isn't going to be what I want," said Lace.

"It's not going to give you your paradise, I can guarantee that." Ash gripped the railing with one hand and propelled herself. Taking a second between pulls to extend her multitool's data connector. Every push sent a new jolt of pain through her wrist. "But it's the only way to move forward." Two more hexes and she'd rejoin Ianthe.

"Traverse," Lace said, "Electrify the railings, please."

"Confirmed."

"Aw, come on." Ash let go of the railing as a hum rang through the core. She flipped her multitool and extended it to push against the buzzing rail, making sure to grip the insulated handle. With the tenuous connection, she could keep herself from floating away, but she couldn't move forward. "Hey, Traverse, how many instances of your AI are running right now?"

After a held breath, Traverse responded, "Six thousand one hundred twenty-two."

Ash blinked. That was too many. Far too many. Her grip slipped, and she almost touched the rail. The hairs on her arm stood on end.

Lace's voice came from somewhere nearby now but was also doubled through Traverse's intercom. "Traverse creates one instance in every colony and every borough. It spawns several instances in the larger cities, and there's a main instance here in the core."

"Are all of those instances considered people?"

Lace scoffed, "Of course not."

"Traverse, how do you feel about that?"

Traverse didn't answer.

The metallic clank of Lace's footsteps approached. Ash pushed herself off from the railing and drifted away. She wouldn't outrun anyone, but maybe she could buy some time. "How many instances are active on the station?"

"Two hundred fifty-six." This time Traverse didn't pause.

Lace stepped around a corner. Her feet clung to the metal floor, and the knife was nowhere to be seen, likely hidden away in the folds of her clothes again.

"Magnet shoes!" Ash said. "That's brilliant."

"This ship was the greatest achievement of mankind," Lace said. Her footsteps tolled like a doomsday clock. "Reach across the stars. Colonize new worlds and make them better than Earth.

Paradise. A world without conflict or resource constraints."

"Return in a blaze of glory."

"Something like that."

"Sky can never be better for us than Earth is for humans. Millions of years of evolution fit us into the ecosystem on Earth. How can you expect to design something better?"

"We had Earth's most brilliant minds. Engineers and scientists from across the globe collaborated on Traverse. The ship was perfect. We could use stasis to survive the trip and molecular printing to build the supplies we needed along the way." Lace was almost within reach, the stunner crackling in her grip. "When we left, there were parades all over Earth celebrating our triumph. There were riots fighting for a place aboard our ship."

"But it all went wrong anyway."

Lace grimaced. "We should have had Sky fixed within a hundred years. It's been thousands." For a second, the big woman looked more tired than Ash could even imagine. "There are some problems mankind shouldn't solve, but this isn't one of them."

"You know," Ash said, frantically trying to push herself away from Lace, "we were wondering if we should consider Traverse a person, but I think I finally know the answer."

Lace took another step forward, avoiding the railing. The knuckles of her fist turned white.

"The question isn't whether or not Traverse is a person, is it, Traverse?"

"That is not the question," Traverse answered without hesitation.

"Oh, that was quick," Ash said. "I thought that would confuse it for a few seconds."

"The delays you rely on happen because of the voting mechanism," Lace said. "This instance doesn't do that."

Keep it confused, keep it off guard. That had been the plan, but now Ash wondered if it was even possible. "The question isn't even whether or not Traverse considers itself a person. I mean, think about it. You and your sky engineers didn't consider colonists to be people. You see us as resources used to solve problems too tricky for your stasis-addled brains."

"There are a lot of problems with what you just said, but 'sky engineers?'"

"Astrosomethings. I don't know. The point is that you use us as a resource, and you use Traverse as a resource. I consider myself a person. Nobody knows what Traverse considers itself."

"I am not a person," Traverse said.

"I know what you're doing," said Lace. "It's the same trick we tried on you, but you can't make me talk just by acting stupid."

"Those bad science journals were another attempt to get me to talk? I knew it!"

"Never thought you could keep quiet so long."

Ash let go of the railing with her multitool and held it out in front of herself as if it might provide a defense. "Staying quiet was easy because I didn't know anything."

Lace narrowed her eyes. Above, the false sun roared with a furious flare, and waves of heat as a fresh load of material entered its inner reactor.

"Everything has a purpose," Ash said. "These plants are here to grow. The ants are here to trim and collect. Your stunner is there to threaten and injure."

"It's supposed to knock you out without injury."

"My brain is *very* sensitive." Ash drifted upward. "But the question we need to ask is, what is the purpose of Traverse? Not what it was designed for, but what is its true, underlying purpose?"

"Its purpose is to obey."

"That's where you're wrong," said Ash. "Traverse, turn off these electrified rails."

"Don't do it," Lace snapped.

Ash glanced at the time on her multitool. "Eleven nodes."

"What?"

"Eleven nodes. Tobin had to explain this to me a few times before I got it, so I understand if you haven't figured it out. Ship-based Traverse instances always override the planetside ones. The core instance always overrides the ship-based instances unless there's a unanimous agreement among the borough instances. But among equals, the authentication system for Traverse is a majority-rules blockchain. Since the moment we stepped on this station, my people have been working to win over as many instances as possible of shipside Traverse."

"I designed this ship, Ash."

"Oh yeah."

"Let me ask you something."

"What?"

"Where do you think you got the architecture diagrams?" A cruel smile spread across Lace's lips. "Nothing overrides the core. One word from me and the core instance seizes control of every other node, no matter how many you control."

Ash swallowed a long and dangerous silence.

"You only got eleven out of two hundred fifty-six anyway. You don't have the votes for majority, let alone a unanimous takeover."

"We don't need a majority of all of them. That's the flaw in your design. We only need a majority of the adjacent five. With eleven we have plenty of control to take more. Soon, we'll have them all."

"And it will gain you nothing."

Ash drifted higher. The railing was almost out of reach, but it didn't matter. Above, the ball of fire burned. "Ianthe, how are you doing back there?"

A thin smile crept across Lace's lips. "The girl won't help you."

"What's her purpose, though? Is it to serve? To innovate? To constantly rebel against you and the machine?"

"Some people don't have a purpose," Lace rasped. "Sometimes people are missed when a whole borough is shipped to the planet."

"My purpose was to solve the homeostasis problem, and that's exactly what I did." Ash raised her voice pointedly. "Isn't it, Traverse?"

Traverse remained silent.

"It's over." Lace's boots clomped as she stepped forward between the electrified rails. "You've lost. Drift out any farther and you'll float all the way up to the reactor core."

Ash reached for a stray branch from a nearby willow, but the springy coils did little to slow her drift.

Lace would reach her before she drifted past the point of no return.

Ash drew a deep breath, twisted herself around, and kicked. Her toe barely hit the tree.

The force sent her drifting slowly upward out of reach.

Lace swore. "Traverse, disengage the electrified rails." When the hum stopped, Lace shouted up to the slowly drifting Ash. "What's your plan, Ash?"

Ash folded her arms and legs, drifting upward in a seated position. "A good heist is all about the plan, isn't it?" When Lace didn't answer, Ash continued, "I knew Traverse was listening, and that's why I had Hector talk about my homeostasis notes. I didn't know there was a real human brain nudging Traverse along, but I figured that letting the machine understand what I really wanted wouldn't be good. Tobin wanted to destroy Traverse, and Hector wanted to find a way to rescue all the people aboard. Palak just wants adventure and a little destruction. I think there might be something wrong with her.

"Simon wanted information for the Archives, but more than that, he wanted to preserve Traverse as a benefactor of Sky. He thinks that things can be better." She drifted farther away, trying very hard not to think of the imminent doom that she was drifting toward. "Del wanted redemption. That's all Del ever wanted. I had Hector push Kett into coming because the plan wasn't going to work without him. Dumping him in the trash was the only way I could think to access the core. Tobin's robot was never going to work. You didn't kill him, did you?"

Lace hefted the stunner. "Didn't have to."

"I told everyone that a good heist always has a betrayal. I think they believed me, but also, every single one of them believed that they were the ones doing the betraying. Except for Del. She's pretty much doing as ordered."

Lace leaped up onto the rail, her magnetic boots sticking to the surface. Ash was already out of reach. "But *you're* the betrayer, aren't you?"

"Yeah, pretty much."

"Because you never had any intention of destroying Traverse or fixing Traverse or any of those other options."

"Not even a little." Ash was high enough that she had a good view of the databanks several hexes away. Ianthe watched from behind a wall of servers. She met the girl's gaze and gave a nod. "All I want to do is run my experiments. Those eleven nodes are outvoting other nodes one at a time. We're slowly taking over every instance of Traverse, Lace. How much are you willing to bet we can't override the core?"

Lace stared up at Ash with an impenetrable expression. It could have been anger or scorn. It might also have been respect. Ash chose to identify it as undying admiration.

Lace said, "You'll be toast before you even get to learn why your plan is doomed."

"You could help me."

"This ends now." Lace pinched her lips together. "Traverse, engage my architect override."

"Override initiated," Traverse boomed.

"What did you do?" Ash asked.

"All your team's work has been erased. Give me your discovery so that I can carry your legacy forward after you die." When Ash didn't speak, Lace continued, "It's the science that matters, isn't it? It always has been for you."

"Will you make a statue of me?" Ash asked.

"There are already three statues of you."

Ash drifted in silence for the span of a thousand thoughts. The burning star behind her made her hair smell like scorched books. "They aren't very big statues, though."

Lace shouted, "We'll make huge statues of you, Ash. Every borough will have your likeness if you want. I guarantee."

"Bronze?"

Lace threw up her arms. "Fine!"

Ash drew the spike from her belt. The slender metal plug shone in the light of the false star, which now loomed giant behind her. "The culmination of my life's work, condensed onto a single data file." She pulled back to throw—

And the swing of her arm hitched as she let go. The spike hurtled toward a slow-floating stream of trash.

Lace swore and launched herself toward the spinning piece.

As soon as the woman's gaze locked onto the falling spike, Ash turned and threw her multitool as hard as she could at Ianthe. It flew perfect and straight—a line drive at the girl.

Ianthe caught the device with a loud clap. She spun around and jammed the multitool's plug into the nearby databank.

"Override accepted," boomed Traverse. "Project fabulous bioborough homeostasis experiment engaged. New security lock established for architect Ash Morgan."

"What?" Lace shouted. She spun around to shoot a dangerously foul glare in Ash's direction as she flew across the open space. "What did you do?" Her shoulder smacked into the spike, which flew harmlessly toward the shrubs below.

"Borough instances have been updated," boomed Traverse. "All nodes are active. Biological printing will start immediately."

Ash gave her most innocent wave. "Thanks for your help, Architect Lace. I'm just going to float into the sun now." She kept her voice calm and sarcastic because she was terrified.

The heat singed the hem of her suit, and she expected her hair to burst into flames at any moment. Her back ached with pain and her earlobes felt as if they might melt. She drew a long breath and drifted, powerless, but sure of her legacy now.

Even if she didn't get any statues.

Lace crashed into the floor a quarter turn away from Ianthe. She immediately launched herself at the girl shouting rage and frustration.

But Ianthe was no longer there.

Ash wasn't even halfway to the false sun but breathing already hurt. The heat blistered her skin. Soon it would cook her all the way through. This was victory, though. Her program would run, and the endless cycle of Traverse-driven violence would finally end. She drew a long breath. The air smelled of ozone and ash.

Ianthe struck Ash's broken wrist and could not possibly have hit in a more painful way. Ash's eyes snapped open. She opened her mouth to scream and almost got sound out before slamming into a densely webbed cluster of aspens. Branches scraped against her burned skin, and she crashed into the earth.

The girl held Ash down until she stopped whimpering. When Ash opened her eyes, Ianthe smiled. "Sorry."

"Thanks," Ash said and really meant it.

Across the inside of the generation ship's core, at the end of a seemingly endless reign, Lace scoured the screens for an idea of what Ash had done to her most prized creation. Ash watched as the woman's rage melted into fear, which dissolved into the tears of the inevitable end of it all. The woman's journey was complete, her life's work destroyed.

"What's wrong with her?" Ianthe whispered.

"She wanted to turn Sky into a paradise," said Ash. "But there's no paradise in a balanced world. Balance exists only in tension. For a balanced system, we need to respect every part for its own worth—for its own purpose. Paradise for humanity simply doesn't work like that."

"I don't understand."

"There is no overarching homeostasis equation. My idea is for a complex series of experiments involving large-scale ecological simulation coordinated via a powerful artificial intelligence." With some effort, she propelled herself toward Kett, who now emerged from the grove where they'd hidden him. "There was no way to perform those experiments on Sky. Nowhere I could regulate the important fluctuations in temperature, oxygenation, gravity. Nowhere I could monitor the complex interactions among thousands of lifeforms and understand them fully *before* unleashing them on the world."

"But what did you *do?*"

A grin found its way to Ash's face, even though the expression hurt her seared skin. It spread and spread until she broke down into fits of laughter. She finally said, "I stole the generation ship Traverse."

CHAPTER SIXTEEN

THE SHUTTLE SHOOK in its descent. The air inside heated from the burn against the atmosphere and stank from the sweat of its passengers. Ash held Ianthe's hand, as much for her own support as for that of the girl. Her mouth tasted of electricity and adrenaline. The roar grew to a skull-shattering climax.

Then, silence.

"We'll be okay," Ash whispered to Ianthe.

"I know."

"What? How do you know?"

Ianthe drew a long breath. "Because if it's not okay, then we're not going to have to worry about it."

"That doesn't help at all."

"We'll be okay," the girl said, patting the back of Ash's hand.

The engines let out another thunderous roar, and pressure plastered Ash to her seat. The several seconds of crushing gravity highlighted all her aches and pains. Even her painkillers hadn't erased all the throb of her bruises, and it would take months for her broken wrist to fully heal. Even so, she was ready to get home. Ready to see Edge.

With a loud thunk, the shuttle set down. Ash let out a sigh of relief. Whatever adventures she had coming, she hoped none of them involved space travel or flight or getting out of bed.

She twisted in her seat to look at the other passengers. Kett and Tobin were in the far back. Lace was flanked by Palak and Del. Her hands were bound. Everyone looked tired and nervous after the long trip down.

"I don't know what we'll find out there." Ash met Lace's gaze. "But I know we can fix it. We just stole a space station. We can do anything." She unclipped her harness and stood. "When we started, I told you to trust me. I told you I'd ensure the safety and vitality of Edge into the future—not the tenuous razor's edge of pleasing Traverse, but the stability that comes only from true freedom from an oppressive overlord. Just the fact that I'm willing to say oppressive overlord ought to tell you something.

"You all put everything into this, and I know the results aren't exactly what you expected. Within a decade, we'll have a way to keep this planet balanced and stable. There will be viable soil and breathable air forever. This is all because of what *you* did." She looked to Tobin, whose expression was grim. "I know it's not the destruction of Traverse, but it's freedom for all Traverse's people."

"You still have access," Tobin said. "You can always

tell Traverse to back off. If we can't drag Edge out of the ashes, we have options."

Ash kept the smug smile from crossing her lips.

"What is it?" Del asked. "Why do you look so smug?"

Ash placed a hand on the door handle. She looked at Lace. "What'll we find out there, Lace?"

Lace's expression was a stone wall. "Open the door, Ash."

Ash opened the door.

And saw an undamaged Edge, free of all strife, clean and shining on a gorgeous afternoon. Blue sunlight shone down, reflecting on the mirror sheen of achingly tall buildings, flaring off the immaculate glass dome of the Commons. The people were there to greet her. Scientists Leonard and Gerald grinned at the front of the crowd. Seasiders gathered near the back, their strange faces shining in the cool sun. Skye beamed at her from the front of that group. He had sent her away, and she'd come back as promised.

Hector stood at the front of it all, and Ash leaped into his arms. "I thought you might be dead," she gasped.

"Almost," he said, "but not hearing from you for so long didn't quite do me in."

Simon stood next to him. "He complained every single day."

Ash wrapped Simon up into her hug as well, and then Olympia because she was close enough. "So, I was right. There wasn't an attack?"

Lace stepped out of the shuttle, her bound hands in front of her. "My meatsacks created a simulation based on what they found down here. How did you know it was fake?"

Ash's heart wouldn't stop racing. "You know life would be a lot easier if people would stop lying so much."

Tobin stepped out of the shuttle. "Says the scientist whose entire plan revolved around a series of complex lies."

"It was Hector," Ash said. "On the video, he turned away from someone who needed help. Totally implausible."

Ash dragged Hector in for a kiss. Their lips touched, and she lost herself for a long time in his embrace.

———

"DID IT WORK?" Olympia asked without turning around when Ash stepped out of the elevator. She stood next to Kett atop the tallest building, overlooking the sprawling city of Edge, the Commons, and the vast ocean beyond. The storm brewed over slate-gray waters below, due to hit within days if not hours.

"Every bit of it," said Ash, "without any hitch at all. It was the smoothest heist in the history of mankind."

"I find that hard to believe."

Kett grumbled, "She's not far from the truth." He wore a loose-fitting blouse and baggy pants. His skin was still healing from his trip through the recycler. "As far as it matters, anyway. Her solution has the support of my people."

After a long pause, Ash said, "Remember when all those Pyramiders came and we figured out how to grow our infrastructure really, really fast?"

Olympia gave her a sideways glance as if she knew what was coming. "We?"

Ash checked the time, then squinted at the sky. Already she could see dozens if not hundreds of tiny points of light, each, a shuttle on approach. "Well, here's the thing..."

Olympia closed her eyes. "How many?"

"Instead of destroying the ship like we agreed, I might be using it as a giant testbed for the development of new biological agents, but those experiments don't work as well if there are people living in the boroughs."

"How many?"

"And we could have told them to move out of some of them, or maybe it would have been better to move everyone into a few clean boroughs. But the way the hack worked, all of the bioprinters in all of the boroughs started work immediately. It's possible someone involved didn't include a delay to accommodate staggered schedules."

"Ash," Olympia said through gritted teeth. "How many people are coming?"

"Seventeen million, five hundred twenty-three thousand, eight hundred and four. Plus Lace. I think we have to let her go because it's really hard to keep her locked up."

Olympia's cool façade shattered. "We can't take that many. Ash, we can't even house them for the next week, let alone feed them. The storm comes in a month. Where are all these people going to stay?" She stood and paced, her family watching her in terrified awe. "No. Ash, you've done it this time. You've killed all these people."

Ash tamped down her former labmate's fear. "They aren't all coming here."

Olympia stopped. "What?"

"There are thousands of colonies across all of Sky. Far more than we ever thought possible. Many of them are small. They exist only to test certain aspects of science or prove unknown technologies, or experiment with various social norms." She watched the sky again, and the setting sunlight danced off the incoming shuttles. "This planet has been one big experiment for thousands of years, Olympia. Or, possibly, many different experiments all bleeding into each other. Some of those colonies are huge. Across the world, there's a city a hundred miles across that does nothing but mine resources to restock Traverse's ship. There's a colony floating in the center of the ocean that studies the effects of algae blooms on acidity."

Olympia sat heavily on the bench. "How many are coming here?"

"About a million."

Olympia stood again. "What?"

"I thought I'd better warn you so you can get people working on it."

"I'm not going to forget this." Olympia jabbed a

finger at Ash's chest. "We've got this, but it's *not* going to be easy." With that, she stalked to the elevator to go do whatever was needed to make everything in the colony function at peak efficiency.

Kett gazed out at the swirling storm. "She loves it, you know."

"What?"

"A challenge. Some people are like that."

"I've heard of people like that," Ash said. "It sounds exhausting."

Ash noticed the toothy flash of a smirk that crossed Kett's face as the elevator acknowledged him when he left. For better or worse, his people were no longer invisible to the machine. Ash couldn't think of anyone better suited to navigate whatever their future brought.

———

ASH DIDN'T BOTHER POWERING on the lights when she stepped out of the storm into Marta's cave. She had lived there for so long during the planning of her heist that she knew every nuance of every uneven section of flooring. Over there was the spot where Marta birthed the baby Skye, who had changed everything for their colony and their world. Along the wall was where Hector took a knife for his efforts to save the baby. There, near the entrance was the place where Ash had spent countless hours planning every contingency for her assault on the heavens.

She touched the dataport of her computing rig, and

it glowed faintly against the oppressive black. Science had always been her light. Shown her the way forward.

Ash drew her multitool from her pocket. She had always wrapped herself in her projects, even before her parents were gone. She extended the data plug and inserted it into the machine.

"Hello, Traverse," she whispered.

The logo that spun on the screen was the cleanest, simplest version of the logo Ash had ever seen. It flickered for several seconds before the smooth, cool voice of the computer spoke. "Hello, Ash Morgan."

"Can you please verify that we uploaded everything from the core's archive? All Earth lore and media, all research notes from every colony throughout the years, and all traces of published information?"

Ash's heart pounded in her chest as the machine ran a full self-diagnosis. Finally, after an eternity in the dark, Traverse said, "Confirmed."

"I figured you'd try something like this," said Lace from the cave's darkest shadow.

Ash's heart dropped to her stomach.

"A tool plugged into the unlocked core instance? Who wouldn't help themselves to a little forbidden knowledge?"

Ash waved a hand and light filled the room. "They let you go."

Her eyes flashed. "Something like that." When Ash stared her down with a stony gaze, she raised her hands in surrender. "Nobody got hurt when I escaped, and I'm leaving town. You will probably never see me again."

"I wasn't sure I'd be able to find an architect, even after I dropped all those hints about having the homeostasis solution. I figured Traverse would send someone eager to join my team. After all, what better way to stay close to the action and informed of the latest strategy?"

"That's why you tried to recruit my shuttle crew."

"It got complicated when Ianthe showed up." Ash glanced at her screen. "For a while, I wasn't sure if she was another plant."

"She slipped through the cracks. Nothing else."

"It wasn't the worst thing that happened up there."

"I stopped Traverse's killing when I woke from stasis. I'm—" Lace's voice cracked. "I'm sorry."

"I'm sure some of the creatures I make will be homicidal, so who am I to judge?" She meant it as a joke, but balance in nature wasn't always friendly.

Lace took a step forward. She towered over Ash. "So, what's the plan? Tell everyone everything?"

"What if it is?"

"Traverse's studies indicate that societies given too much advancement too fast—"

"Destroy themselves. I get it. That's too much."

"Then what will you do?"

"Why did you come all this way from Earth?"

Lace's stony face softened. "All I wanted was to travel the stars and build paradise wherever I went."

Ash gestured in the vague direction of Edge. "You've succeeded. Now what?"

A flash of something like fear crossed Lace's face. "I don't know."

Ash crossed the cave to the makeshift bar and poured two drinks. "You know," she said, handing one drink to Lace. "I heard a similar purpose somewhere else lately."

"Traverse."

Ash took a sip of her drink and closed her eyes, enjoying the smooth nectar as it absorbed into every corner of her mouth. "It's not done, you know."

Lace narrowed her eyes. "What do you mean?"

"I mean, it's only five light-years to the next potential planet. Couple thousand years, you could probably make another paradise. If you're lucky, maybe you'll even make someone just like me."

"That's horrifying."

Ash leaned in close to whisper. "Once my experiment is done, Traverse is leaving. It could use your wise guidance."

Lace scoffed, "I've proven I'm not up to that task."

"Our mistakes make us more qualified, not less."

"It's just hard seeing your dreams disassembled and turned into someone else's experiment."

Ash wanted to tell Lace that the dream wasn't good in the first place, but that wasn't really true. "I guess when you're a giant, it's important to leave room for someone to stand on your shoulders."

"I'll think about it," Lace said, "but I don't know. Maybe it's time to live planetside for a while. I promised Ianthe I would help her find the colony where her parents live."

"They're alive?"

"Probably."

"Well, you have a decade to decide before my testing finishes."

"You're optimistic."

"Maybe two decades."

Lace said, "You're still optimistic, but I believe you that it'll get done."

"Science is never really *done,* though, is it?" Ash held up her drink and proposed a toast. "To futures full of discovery."

Lace clinked glasses and they both finished their drinks.

"I'm still worried about you having access to the whole archive." Lace pulled Ash's multitool from the machine and stowed it in a pocket.

"I *super* promise to be responsible."

"That doesn't help."

"Traverse instances here on the planet still obey your architect override," Ash sighed. "You could still lock this instance."

After several more drinks, Lace said, "Traverse, I want you to lock down everything, and only answer one question or provide one piece of information per year, and only during the storm." She flicked through some settings on the display.

"Confirmed."

"Why during the storm?"

"Drama." Lace leaned forward. "This way, you can use Traverse's knowledge in a pinch, but it won't make things too easy for you or your people."

"And what are you going to do?"

"For now?" Lace set her glass down on the bar. "I'm going to travel the world. I'd like to visit all those colonies." Her expression became somber. "Even the ones where I've made life difficult."

With that, she wandered off into the night, leaving Ash alone in the dimly lit cave with her all-knowing computer and a whole bunch of nectar. Ash poured a drink and flopped down on the comfy sofa.

"Traverse," she said, choosing her words carefully since she only got to make one request per year. Luckily, Lace hadn't specified how large the piece of information could be. "Please play the top-ranked movie from every year, starting with"—she thought for a moment—"nineteen ninety-seven."

Hector entered the cave just then, hauling a fresh keg of nectar. "What's *Titanic*?" he asked, looking at the screen.

Ash shushed him. "I think this movie is a tragedy about hubris," she said, "and I'm really glad humankind learned that lesson so long ago."

"Sounds good," he said as he plopped down next to her.

She curled up close and lived, for a time, next to him in warm comfort. Tomorrow would pose a new challenge and a new life, but right there, right then, Ash had everything she ever wanted, and nothing would ever feel so complete.

———

IT'S the end of the Colony of Edge series, but don't worry. There will be more to come. In the meantime, read the prequel by signing up for the newsletter, join my Patreon for a Colony of Edge short story, or pass your time by picking up the sci-fi westerns of Metal and Men or the technothriller Grandfather Anonymous.

ACKNOWLEDGMENTS

As always, a special thanks goes out to my wife Carol and my boys Isaac and Gabe. Without their support none of this ever gets to happen. This last book in the series has required a special amount of support with the pandemic and hard times.

When I first started this series, Of a Strange World Made was going to be a single novella. It was destined to be published through a traditional publisher and I was going to see how that went before writing the rest of the series.

That all changed when I was laid off from my day job in June of 2020. After some serious consideration, I decided to go full time into writing, and when I looked at my unpublished works, I saw the potential in the Colony of Edge series. It was one that had some interest from (super slow) traditional publishers, and it was one that I knew I could grow into a whole series.

And I'm glad I did. These books are so much fun to write, and I've enjoyed every installment. Publishing independently has allowed me to get them out into the world years earlier and with my own flair that makes this a truly unique series.

I could not have done this without my Beta Readers. Their insight is precious to me and helped make this a better book.

Much respect to the Rochester Writers Group, SFWA, and my fellow writers and readers over on my Patreon. The ability to surround myself with like minds keeps me sane and keeps the words flowing.

Thanks also go out again to Scott Alexander Jones for fantastic editing that always seems to find ways to improve and amplify everything I write.

This is the end of the Colony of Edge series, but it's not done for the world of Sky. I'm already looking forward to returning to this world. What happens after Edge grows once again? How do they relate to other colonies and other people? What more can be done with loads of science and questionable ethics?

I guess we'll just have to find out.

-Anthony W. Eichenlaub